Uglies of the Beauty Salon
2
STILL UGLY
Ms. BBC

ISBN- 978-0-692-75531-0

Editor Joan Stanford

Second BBC Promotions paperback edition 2015

10 9 8 7 6 5 4 3 2

Cover design and graphic design: BBC Promotions & Ashley Cunningham of Image Mart

DEDICATION

This book is dedicated to My Mo Bunny,
King Shug, and all my supporters.

I'M MOTHER NATURE

I am strength, and struggle, with my mind I create greatness, destroy in bounds, and manifest inspiration, my essence shines light in the darkened places beyond reach.
A woman, who am I.
My tears embrace the universe when I'm happy, sad, in love, or angry. Powerful, but also fragile, I birth kings and queens from prides to thrones. Notice diamonds in the rough.
Touch them from my spirit without anything in return.
A woman, who am I.
Gathering massive storms, cleansing the children of pain and suffering. Wanting to feed my fellow man who has appeared hungry, not with food but with mental nourishment. Seducing with ultimate beauty from my inner loins.
Growing limbs of wisdom, willing to give back all that I absorb. Releasing passion to the unworthy and continuing to stand strong.
A woman, who am I.
Taking to be misused, abused, and ignored
The beauty of being a blessing, I never distance from my destiny, able to give the earth the nutrients it hungers for. Afraid and fearless. Injecting love, pouring emotions and gratitude into each body I come across believing we shall all live as great as we are born to do.
A woman, who am I. #BBC
All women are queens, mothers of the earth. If you know nothing else, know your worth.
I'm #BBC and I am Mother Nature! #LongLiveTheEmpress

CHAPTER 1

BEEP, BEEP, BEEP…
HONK, HONK, HONK…
Doodoodoodoodo, doodoodoodoodo, doodoodoodoodo…

The machines and medical devices all alarmed at the same time with flashing lights and numbers as Biggie jumped up out of her coma. The alarms sent a panic to the nurses' station, which happened to be right in the front of Biggie's hospital room.

One nurse dressed in lavender colored scrubs with a Betty Boop cover jacket was having her third cup of coffee for the day because she worked a sixteen-hour double and was having trouble staying awake. Startled by the alarms, she jumped up and her coffee went flying into the air. Another nurse, who wore the older style nurse's uniform, a short white skirt with white shoes and nude stockings, was having her daily secret love affair conversation on the main hospital phone. She giggled with the doctor from another floor while she twirled her strawberry blonde hair with one finger. For the last five minutes, she had been smiling at the sexual advances he was making over the phone in his sneaky voice. He had to whisper since he happened to be married to the director of the hospital board and he did not want anyone to hear their conversation.

But when the alarms sounded, she hopped up from the desk and left the phone dangling from the desk. Another nurse was actually doing her job, going through paperwork of patients who were already released from ICU. All three nurses stumbled over each other, then ran in and tried to restrain a limp but strong body. Biggie was causing an uproar as she snatched out her breathing tubes and IVs while flopping her arms and lifting herself out of the medical bed.

The bruises Peaches left on Biggie after she beat her into coma for sleeping with her husband were filled with blood. Biggie's eyes were barely able to open and her lips were swollen beyond their maximum stretch. However, she was able to scream out, what brought her out of her coma in the first place.

"I know who did it! I know who did it! Get off me! Get off me. I know who did it. I know who killed G-mama. Please help me. Where are my girls? Where are they? I know who did it!" Biggie cried out with massive tears rolling down her bruised face.

But the nurses were not listening. They just wanted to make sure they calmed her down and fixed the damage she caused by snatching out her lines.

One nurse demanded to another nurse, "Get the straps!"

Another nurse ran to the nurses' cabinet, retrieved the straps and ran them back to the bed where all the nurses fought to try to get Biggie sedated and calmed. Before they could get a needle ready, Biggie struck one of the nurses across the face.

"Oh shit!" Secret lover nurse yelled out. Not only was she pissed that Biggie slapped her, but she had a hot date with her married doctor and she wanted to be as pretty as she could for him.

Dee, who was waiting in the family room, saw all the commotion and ran to the entrance phone, and ordered to be let in. Dee began banging on the doors, screaming for someone to open the doors. She had a feeling something was wrong with Biggie. A nurse from the other unit ran around to see what all the banging was about. She immediately saw Dee pounding her fists like crazy. She went behind the nurses' station, picked up the phone and pointed her finger to the entrance phone for Dee to go and pick it up.

Dee, while jerking her head back and forth like a ghetto girl and pointing her finger, yelled, "If you don't open this motherfuckin' door right now I'm gonna kick this bitch in and then kick your ass for being so stupid!"

The nurse must have read Dee's lips, because she pushed the button and walked off to her unit like she didn't know what was going to happen next. When Dee finally entered the hallway, she heard all the screaming. And when she hit the corner to Biggie's room, all she saw was a big manly nurse strapping down her now awake friend. A nurse was on top of Biggie's bed straddling her to hold her down. Another nurse had blood in her hands and there were medical tubes everywhere, which sent Dee into a little state of shock. She stayed there for a matter of seconds until she was brought back by Biggie's yell.

"I know who did it! I know who killed G-mama!" Biggie repeatedly screamed out.

Dee shouted, "Hey! What the hell are you doing to her?"

I'm sorry, you can't be in here right now!" one nurse cried while trying to get strap ties onto Biggie's arms.

"You got me fucked up! If you don't get your hands off her, I'm going to tie your ass down! And believe me, you're not going to like it either," Dee warned.

"Excuse me!" the nurses' eyes darted at Dee.

"You heard me." Dee's eyes darted back. She then tuned into her friend's cries. She suddenly made out what she was screaming and chill bumps crawled up on her arms. She literally felt chills run down her back and fear build up in her stomach.

Dee's mind began to fill with thoughts. *"What does she mean she knows? Did she remember something? Could she know? How would she know? Has someone been in this room with her while they were gone? Maybe she had a nightmare while in her coma and she didn't know she was awake now?"*

"Wait. Stop! Stop!" Dee yelled.

"I know who did it! I know who did it! G, I'll save you. I, I, I'll save you, G-mama!" Biggie began to calm down, but was still agitated.

Dee realized Biggie was not aware of her surroundings and was just dreaming or hallucinating. What she hadn't realized was that the nurses had given Biggie a sedative and it switched her from assuring thoughts to mixed up thoughts and emotions.

Dee sat down in the chair beside Biggie's bed and let the nurses finish observing her friend. Tears rolled down her face, as thoughts of guilt consumed her heart and made her mind race. She could do nothing but sigh as a boat of tears ran into her hands. She wanted to scream out, "Why god? Why is this happening?" But she just sobbed and cried so hard it hurt her soul. She sniffled as she felt hands on her shoulders. Without looking, she knew who it was by the scent of his cologne and the strength of his touch.

"Jeremiah," Dee muttered through the tears and hurt.

"Baby, is everything alright? I came back from the cafeteria with the coffee and food and you were gone. I saw all the nurses gone from the desk, then I saw them all running back and forth. What happened? Did she wake up? Did something go wrong? What are they doing to her? Baby, talk to me."

Dee could not speak. Even if she could, she didn't know what to say because she wasn't sure herself. She just cried while leaning her head to lie on Jeremiah's hands.

Jeremiah stood there staring in wonder at Biggie while the nurses did their jobs. With every pull and jerk from the nurses as they tried to make Biggie comfortable as she fell into her sedation, Dee's body jerked too. Although her friend couldn't feel any pain, Dee could feel it for her. She knew they were only doing their jobs, but they were being overly rough. It was already hurting her from her insides to see the things her friend, had already endured.

Jeremiah wanted to take Dee out of there, fearing it was too much for her and the baby. But he knew she wouldn't leave and would be pissed at him for asking her to do so. Although he didn't like her friends, he really felt bad about everything Dee was going through and wanted to be as supportive as he could. He just massaged her shoulders, stayed quiet and continued to be there for her like he had been doing for the last five days.

After the nurses were all done, the strawberry blonde nurse turned to Dee and whispered in a sweet southern voice. "You have fifteen minutes and then we really have to ask you to please wait in the family room. She really needs her rest and we have to shut down the floor for rounds. When we're back up in two in a half hours someone will come and get you and you can sit in here until visiting hours are over." She smiled then walked out the room, patting the other nurses on the back.

Dee stood up and stumbled a bit, weakened from all the emotion and crying. Jeremiah caught her arm and helped her to stand. She never turned to look back and thank him. She just wanted to touch Biggie's hand, feel her spirit and love on her family. As she moved closer to the bed, she began to tear up again. Her knees weakened and her heart began to beat faster and faster. She couldn't control her breathing and began to feel faint. She grabbed onto the bed rail and looked down at her beaten friend then whispered in a teary voice, "Biggie, I don't know if you can hear me, but I'm here." Dee cried some more then began again. Her mouth opened, but her words struggled to come out through the pain. "I, I, I'm sorry for what I let happen to you, G-mama and Peaches. It's all my fault." Her cry deepened. "I was supposed to protect you guys. I promised God if he blessed me with a family, I would love them, protect them, and never let anything happen to them. Ooohhhhhhh, God, I've failed you." Dee fell to her knees and Jeremiah picked her up off the floor and walked her out of Biggie's room.

He thought, *"I should have asked her to leave when I saw what it was doing to her."*

Jeremiah nodded to the nurse that was sitting at the desk to open the doors so he could take Dee to the family room. She obliged with a sad look on her face, wishing there was something she could do to make it a little easier, but she never said a word. Jeremiah walked through the open doors, took Dee in the family room, placed her on his lap and rocked her back and forth. As her face stayed buried in his chest, she cried like a baby for over an hour until she fell asleep.

When Dee awakened she was still on Jeremiah's lap and he had nodded away to sleep. She couldn't believe after all the shit she had been through with him, including the fact he still could be the killer, and everything else, this man was still by her side. She didn't know why, but among all the emotions inside of her— anger, fear, frustration, and guilt— there was passion. Out of the blue she kissed him softly on his lips, which woke him up. He wiped his mouth, thinking he had drooling. He looked at Dee and she had a different look on her face. He didn't know what it meant, but he knew something had changed in the beautiful woman he had rocked to sleep.

"Are you okay, baby?" Jeremiah smirked in wonder.

Dee didn't answer. She kissed him again, this time with a little more passion and much harder than the first time. This time she made a deep, intense sound, which made Jeremiah's dick stand hard and strong. He began to feel guilty and thought, *maybe this isn't what she needs right now.* He tried to think of everything to make his erection go down, but Dee wasn't letting up. Right in the family room where another couple sat on the other side of the wall, Dee turned her body around on Jeremiah's lap and straddled. She pressed her pelvic to his hard muscled stomach as she slid in she could feel the hardness of his long, throbbing dick move against her moist, yearning, hot pussy.

"Mmmmmm," Dee hummed in her throat and rocked her pelvic back and forth, still not saying a word. She wrapped her arms around Jeremiah's neck and bit his ear lobes softly. She kissed down his neck aggressively while biting lightly into the sides. Jeremiah finally gave in and wrapped his arms around her waist, pulling her in tighter making her wind her hips in a slow grind.

"Aaaahhhhh," Dee purred as she rotated her hips deeper into Jeremiah. His hand went from her waist down to her ass and cuffed it tightly. Dee kissed him in the mouth as deep as she could, sucking on his tongue like it was a lollipop. The couple on the other side of the wall stopped watching television and stared at each other as if they heard gunshots. The guy tried to sit on the other side of their room to see if he could catch a glimpse of what was really going on, but because the door blocked them and the wall was curved from the inside, there was no way for him to see anything without getting up and going to the door. And that's just what he did. His wife gawked at him and shooed him away from the door.

Jeremiah and Dee didn't think one minute about being heard or seen by anyone. They continued to devour each other as if there was no one else around. Jeremiah scooted to the edge of the chair to get more leverage because Dee's "Big voluptuous size 16 pregnant Body" was keeping him from getting into her like he really wanted to. Being on the edge allowed Dee's ass to settle right in his hands and he was able to cup it just the way he wanted to. He pulled Dee's maxi dress up to his cuffed hand and slipped his fingers from the side of her pink lace panties then slid his finger from her asshole very lightly to her clitoris.

"Aaaaaahhhhh" Dee moaned, still never saying two words.

The guy by the door was immediately turned on. He watched as if it was a real life porn show going on right in front of him. His girlfriend started to get upset.

"Everyone else is always more important than me, right? If it's not your stupid friends, it's that damn video game, or your horrible mother. This turns you on, but you haven't touched me in months!"

But the guy ignored her as he rubbed his crotch softly, focusing on Dee's big round black ass. He always had fantasies about being with a black woman. But being a simple white boy from Chardon with only two black people attending his school, it never happened.

Just as he was in deep thought imagining he was the one stroking Dee with her dark brown skin wrapped around his soft milky body, a magazine blasted him on the side of his face. He grabbed the side of his face and winced.

Bam, Bam, Bam! His girl banged on the wall as hard as she could. "Get a room, perverts!"

"What is wrong with you?" the guy questioned. "Why are you being rude? You don't know what these people are going through. This could be their last night on earth or something and you're ruining it for them?"

"Oh, but you watching is not just as invading? What is your problem?" She sighed with disgust.

However, the girl's anger and rage did not shake one nerve in Dee and Jeremiah. As a matter of fact, by the time the guy was back at the door to peek and get his freak on, Jeremiah had scooped Dee up and slammed her against the curved wall on the side of the door where homeboy couldn't see them. Jeremiah had begun to finger fuck Dee with his pointer finger and his middle finger, deep, hard and slow.

Dee's arms stayed tightly wrapped around Jay's neck. Her legs cradled over his arms and her pussy was dripping with her sweet juices all over his fingers, his shoes, and the hospital family room floor.

"Ahhhh, oh shit. Ooooooh, baby, uuummmmm," Dee moaned in a heavy whisper.

"You like that, baby? Damn, this pussy so wet and tight. I miss touching this pussy, baby, damn!" Jeremiah's voice elevated to different heights.
He started unbuckling his pants because he needed to feel the inside of her with more than just his fingers. Just when his pants dropped down to his knees and exposed his rock, hard, long dick, along comes little miss overworked, coffee drinking nurse entering the family room. Shocked, her face turned several shades of red as soon as she entered the room to witness the freak session that was taking place.   "Hmm, hmm." She cleared her throat to

let them know she was in the room, although she was used to plenty going on in this room.

She began speaking as if nothing was going on. "I wanted to let you know we're almost finished with our rounds. Although she is still resting, she is cleaned up and ready for visitors. Give us a few more minutes and you can come in." The nurse tilted her head downward, not giving eye contact and left with a sneaky grin on her face. Dee slid down Jeremiah's body like a fun ride and licked her lips.

Jeremiah was pissed at the interruption. They both adjusted their clothing and sat in chairs across from each other never saying a word. Dee felt embarrassed by her actions. How could she be so free to give herself to this man— a man who could still be the murderer, a man who had beaten her and abused her friends. But she also thought of how he was there for her in her time of sorrow, so she didn't say a word.

Jeremiah wondered what Dee was thinking about, but he dared not ask, afraid to ruin the moment. Just then, they heard a moan. They looked up to the door to see the couple on the other side smashed against the door getting their freak on and both began to laugh.

CHAPTER 2

Peaches walked into Dee's kitchen slopped over and raggedy as all get out wearing her tore up terrycloth sky blue robe with a torn pocket on the right side and the belt missing. Only an extra-large safety pin was holding it closed. She wore this over her mismatched pajamas with one house shoe on one foot and an oversized sock on the other.

She muttered to herself off and on. "I knew it! I knew that bitch was a dirty, funky bitch." Then she stopped in her tracks as if she was talking directly to someone and began again. "Bitch, you gon' fuck my husband? Oh, no, no, no, bitch, not mine. I should've killed that ho is what I should've done. Ummm hmm," she said, answering herself to co-sign on her should've, could've, would've. Suddenly she cried out, "G-mama, I love you, G. Aaahh, I don't know why I treated you like that. Aaahh! Huh? G, is that you?"

She scanned the room to see if anyone was there because she swore she heard a voice. As Peaches walked to the cabinet and pulled out some crackers, she heard another voice, dropped the crackers on the floor and screamed. "G-mama, is that you? Don't scare me!" she cried out again. "G-mama, why you leave me, G?" She waddled back and forth from side to side, never moving her feet from the place she stood in.

She fell back against the counter and pulled a silver and black flask out of her robe pocket that wasn't torn and took a big gulp. She turned the flask to the side and poured some on the Italian marble kitchen floor and began to sing.

"This song's dedicated to my homey and that gansta lean," she slurred and spit as she continued not knowing the words. She waved her hand and walked out of the kitchen through the long hallway, across the foyer until she reached into the living area. She went to sit down on the chaise and flopped right down to the floor. "Oh, excuse me," she said in an apologetic voice, as if she bumped into someone or stepped on their shoes by mistake. When she tried to get up, she struggled and fell again. "Got damn it!" she cried out.

As she tried over and over to get up she heard a vibration coming from across the room on the couch where she had been posted for days. "G? G-mama, is that you?" she said, wiping tears from her face and focusing in on the noise to hear what it was saying to her. "Shhh, shhh. Be quiet. I'm trying to hear G," she said to her imagination.

She crawled across the living area. As she got closer she heard it louder and reached down into the cushion of the powered white couch that matched the chaise she couldn't find herself to sit on minutes ago. She pulled out her cell phone, which she completely forgot about. When she pulled the phone out from between the cushions, she looked at the screen and swallowed a deep gulp. Her heart rate shot up fifty beats and her mind raced a mile a second with her eyes bouncing from one side of her head to the other.

"Hello?" Peaches answered with fear in her voice.

"Peaches," the voice whispered back to her.

"NNNOOOOO, NO, NO, NO, NO. IT CAN'T BE. IT CAN'T BE!" Peaches threw the phone across the living area, jumped up on her feet and said, "Feet, don't fail me now!" She ran out of the living area as fast as she could, screaming and crying and waving her arms like a wild woman. The phone read G-MAMA.

Peaches ran through the foyer and right out the front door, raggedy robe and all. She jumped in the car and placed her face on the steering wheel, holding both sides of it with her hands in a tight grip. Her forehead pushed in so hard that she began to blow the horn without intent, which scared her even more. Although she had been drinking, she was well aware what had happened. Maybe it even sobered her up. She stayed face down on the steering wheel for maybe ten minutes or so, before she gathered up enough courage to peek up and look around to see if someone was watching her or if she left the door opened. But she didn't see anyone and the front door was closed. She looked through the car up over the mirror and in the glove compartment for her extra key. She knew she was not going back in that house and she needed to get as far away as possible. She found the key on the passenger side mirror. As soon as she tilted the flap, it fell down right into her hand. She started the car, without checking her rearview mirror. She put the car in reverse and backed out, not knowing her destination. Her breathing was so strong she couldn't speak. All she knew was she needed to clear her mind to make sense of what just happened. Peaches turned on the radio to relax and shut out the silence. She wanted to get rid of the many thoughts running through her head. She drove for about ten miles before she began to feel herself relaxing, grooving to the music and becoming calm. When she hit her next stop light, she rested back into the driver seat and closed her eyes. She recalled her phone ringing and it being a call from G-mama. Her mind began to race.

What if it was all fake and G was really alive? What if G only wanted to tell her so they could run away together? What if G was in the CIA and they had her on a special mission and she could only tell one person so she called me so that someone would know she was okay? Or what if...

Peaches shook her head to stop herself from going overboard with her thoughts. She saw that the light had changed for her and laughed out loud to herself. "CIA?"

As she began to laugh to herself, and think maybe she really needed to put down the Hennessey and get her mind right, she turned her head to caught a quick glance out the passenger side window and was suddenly staring right into G-mama's face.

"Oh shit!" she yelled while swerving over into the other lane, pushing a teal colored SUV over onto the curb. Peaches took her hands off the steering wheel and threw her hands up over her face with the car still in motion and her foot still on the gas. She ran the car right into the back of a police cruiser. The crash sent her head right into the steering wheel and then flipped her over the driver seat into the back seat.

The police officer jumped out of the passenger side of the vehicle. The shocks from the hit boosted his adrenaline to move lightning fast. His partner ran out of the diner, leaving the two coffees behind.

The officer who had been driving moved up close to the car to see if anyone was inside and if they were hurt.

With each step, he rocked his neck side to side, feeling the pain in his neck from the impact of the hit. His partner pulled his weapon and started up on the other side. Peaches, not fully worried about the crash, peeked up from behind the seat to see if G-mama's ghost was still in the car with her. With blood running from her nose, she popped her head back down when the police banged on the driver side window demanding she step out the car. When the officer opened the door, Peaches started screaming and ranting on about G-mama.

"Officer, I know how this looks, but it wasn't my fault. G-mama died and she called my phone, right? But then I took off because I almost killed my friend, Biggie, not G. She was fucking my husband and I ran that big SUV off the road and the ghost was in the seat and it scared me. She was my lover and my husband found out and beat me up and Dee pregnant because my husband killed her... Ouch! My hheeeaad!"

Peaches passed out in the officer's arms.

When Peaches came to she was in an ambulance handcuffed to a rolling bed and the EMS driver was calling in her condition to the hospital. Another one was sticking a needle in her arm. Peaches was dazed and confused and she drifted back off.

When she woke up again she saw people all in white. She thought she was dead.

"Peaches. Peaches," a voice faintly called her name. She rose up in her hospital bed in a seated position.

"Is someone there?" Peaches called out to the open space.

"Excuse me," she called out to the nurses and doctors, but no one answered her.

"Peaches," the voice called again.

Peaches climbed down out the bed to follow the voice. Everybody seemed to be ignoring her anyway. She walked down the long hallway, walking by each room, but every room she looked in no one was there. She continued walking her bare feet on the cold, white floors and with each step, chills ran up her body.

"Hello? Is anyone there?"

The hall seemed to get longer than it appeared. Peaches came to two double doors that read DO NOT ENTER in big bold red letters. But she could hear voices. She thought that maybe they were the voices that kept calling her. Peaches pushed one of the doors open, only to hear her name slowly being called again. She jumped back, releasing the door and peeked into the square window to see if anyone had noticed. No one moved. There were six doctors standing around, all with hospital masks over their mouths and staring down at a body.

"Peaches," the voice called from the room, sending goose bumps down Peaches' spine.

Peaches pushed the doors open again. She was scared out of her wits, but still needed to know where the voice was coming from. Step by step she dragged herself to the table to see where the voice was coming from and what all the doctors were staring at. When she reached the table, she almost fell off her feet as she saw an opened body showing every organ, with blood and guts everywhere. She covered her mouth and peered at the face of the body to see it was G-mama. G-mama's head snapped to face her.

"Peaches, I love you. Don't' you love me?" G-mama's corpse spoke. Peaches eyes widened with fear. She jumped back into a doctor and when she looked up at him, he was also G-mama. Peaches screamed when he grabbed her. This woke her up. She was still handcuffed to the hospital bed. The nurses were standing over her, taking her blood pressure when she jumped out her unconscious state. The tightness of the cuff felt like the grip the doctor in her dream had on her. The nurse took her small flashlight and opened both of Peaches' eyes to see if she was fully awake and able to follow the light.

"Ma'am, are you with us? Can you follow the light for me, please?" The nurse asked in a patois accent.

Peaches eyes went from left to right as the nurse slowly moved the light from one side of her face to the other.

"Okay, very well, my girl. Now we have some paperwork for you to fill out. First, can you tell me your name?"

Peaches didn't say a word. She knew she was in trouble, but she didn't' know how bad and if Big Rob taught her anything, it was don't answer anything until she knew all the details and right now nothing was making sense to her. So much was blurry to her. She looked around the room, outside in the hall, and at all the nurses and people's faces to make sure she wasn't still dreaming and seeing G-mama.

The police officers were right outside Peaches' room filling out their reports, while flirting with some of the nurses at the same time. You could tell the nurses were familiar with the officers because they were playfully pushing them and smart talking them like they were all old friends. Peaches just laid back on the table, still a bit in shock about what was going on. She wondered if it could all be a dream and maybe she was still asleep. She watched as the nurse walked out to speak to the officers and back around the desk. Still dazed, she turned her head to the wall and cried in her armpit.

An officer entered the room. "Ma'am, my name is Officer Richard Linton. Do you know where you are?" he asked Peaches with a stern voice.

"Yes, sir," Peaches replied through her tears.

"Do you know why you're here?"

"No, no I don't," Peaches whispered.   "Well, ma'am, I'll tell you why you are here. You caused two major accidents, one being with myself and my partner's police cruiser. You admitted to attempt of murder and spoke about seeing ghosts all while you were operating a vehicle under the influence of alcohol." He looked back and forth from his notepad to Peaches' face to see her reaction.   Peaches gasped for breath. She looked out into the hall where the nurses and the other officers were all quiet and trying their best to eavesdrop.

"Ma'am, I have a few questions for you. What is your full name?"

"My name is Sandra Peaches Bryan, but all my friends call me Peaches." She cleared her throat when she said it.

The officer didn't blink an eye as he went on with his line of questioning. "And how old are you, Mrs. or Miss Bryan?"

"I'm thirty years old and its Mrs." Peaches rolled her eyes, mad at the fact she had to clarify that she was married to Big Rob's black ass, which she definitely wasn't going to tell the officer. She just wanted to get out of there and go back to Dee's house.

"I didn't read you your Miranda rights before you fainted." He began. "You have the right to remain silent. Anything you say can be used against you in the court of law…" Peaches' eyes widened. "I'm under arrest?"

CHAPTER 3

Dee was tired and restless. She really wanted Biggie to wake up. She wanted to know if her friend was all right. As she sat on the side of Biggie's bed and held her friend's hand she thought about all the great times they had together at the shop, going shopping, getting to know each other, working together, and crying together. She thought about her mother and "Heavenly Hands," the man who raised her. She began to speak out loud to Biggie about Heavenly.

"You know he was the one who taught me about being a lady." She sniffed her nose as a single tear dropped from her cheek. "He would always say, Dee, baby you are worth a million stars. Collect them all and then demand a million more. One day you're going to have a family that loves you so much you're not going to know where to put all that love." Dee squeezed Biggie's hand as she mocked Heavenly Hands' voice.
She sighed.

"And he was right. I love you guys so much and I believe you all love me too. Sometimes I used to wonder what I would do if I lost any of you. Now I'm here and I don't know what to do. I don't feel like myself. I've already lost G-mama and I feel so bad. If I would have listened to her she would still be alive. How could I treat her like that? I was supposed to be there for her. I know she really didn't have anyone. She loved me with all her heart and I let her get murdered. I'm such a horrible friend. What's the point of wanting to love if I don't even know how to return it? Damn, Biggie, I need you to wake up. I need you to tell me what to do. I need you to tell me it's gonna be all right."

Dee cried out to her friend with deep emotion in hopes that she could pull her out from her sedation, but nothing happened. She stared in Biggie's face silently praying she blinked, twitched or did anything to let her know she was there with her, but Biggie was out like she was still in a coma. The hospital needed her to be that way because of all the bruising and pain she was in. There was no waking her until the medication wore off. Dee didn't say another word. She laid her head on her hand clutched in Biggie's hand on the side of the bed and welp. As tears dropped from her eyes a machine that she didn't notice before started to make a humming sound. Dee lifted her head to see what the machine was doing. It hummed three full times, each time zigzag lines were marked up and down on the paper that rolled from a slot in the machine. Then numbers flashing about stat picked up speed.

"What the hell? What does this mean?" She spoke to no one in particular.
The nurse walked in to check the machine after the third hum.

"Excuse me, is this machine letting us know that she's waking up?" Dee asked with a bit of hope on her face looking into the nurse's eyes.

The nurse tilted her head and gave a sweet smile. "Oh, no, sweetie. This is for us to monitor the baby, so we can make sure that although mommy is in pain, the baby isn't."

Dee's eyes bucked. "BABY! Biggie's pregnant? Oh my God! What the hell?"

"Shhhh. I'm sorry, but you have to keep your voice down. We have people trying to rest," the nurse said with her left pointer finger up to her mouth.

Dee waved her hand and whispered, "Sorry," as she rubbed her own pregnant belly and slid down in her chair. She looked over at Biggie and thought, *you're pregnant by Big Rob, by Peaches' husband Big Rob.*

"Are you okay, Miss? Do you need a cup of water or something? You don't look so well." The nurse walked over to Dee and touched her on her shoulder, while looking her in the face.

Dee looked up at the nurse with a worried glare. "Are you sure she's pregnant? I mean, are you really, really sure she's pregnant?"

"Yes," the nurse swallowed lightly and walked over to the machine. "See? Here's how you can see the details for the baby," the nurse said, pointing to some numbers on the screen. "And here is where we check the breathing and monitor mommy's levels." She is in the early stages of her pregnancy so it is no wonder it's a shock to you. She probably didn't know herself." The nurse tried to comfort Dee with her words. "Would you like me to bring you something to drink or eat?"

"Umm yes, some crackers and ginger ale, please." Dee sat waiting for the nurse to return. Dumbfounded, she sat down in the chair slumped over with her knees together and feet tilted inward to the floor. Lost for words, lost for thoughts she looked from machine to machine and then back to Biggie. She looked out at the nurses' station, where the nurses laughed and joked around with each other, then back to Biggie. She looked at Biggie's belly and back at the machine trying to come up with a thought or something to rationalize the news. However, nothing popped up in her mind. She was completely stumped. There was too much going on in her brain to let anything else get through. Dee pulled her chair closer to the hospital bed, grabbed the extra pillow off the side of the desk and laid her head down slowly as if her brain was going to leak out if she moved too fast. She then took Biggie's free hand and laid it on her face for comfort. *How could this all be happening?* she wondered.

Footsteps walked into the room. Dee lifted her head to see if it was the nurse bringing her crackers and drink back, but it's wasn't the nurse. Based on Dee's surprised eyes, the visitor knew it was a problem. *What the hell is he doing here* she thought to herself. Big Rob walked in with his Boston pro model hat pulled down over his forehead, with sorrow in his eyes and grief on his face. He didn't say a word to Dee as he moved in closer to Biggie's bed. Dee stared at him with fear in her eyes and disappointment across her face.

Big Rob leaned down and kissed Biggie on the cheek. "Damn, baby, I never meant for this to happen to you," he sighed.

Dee still didn't speak a word.

Big Rob looked over at her and attempted to have a conversation with her with his eyes, not knowing how to approach a real conversation. Somehow, Dee knew what he wanted to know. She saw in his eyes that he really cared for Biggie.

"She was in a coma, but then she woke up and she was screaming and throwing a fit so they had to sedate her. She's in a lot of pain and they need her to rest so she doesn't have a miscarriage." Dee darted her eyes at Big Rob to review his reaction to the news.

Rob's head hung low as Dee fed him the details until she said miscarriage. His head shot up and he said, "MISCARRIAGE!"

"Yes, muthafucka, miscarriage. You got your wife's co-worker and once upon a time friend pregnant! How could you? This shit is all your fault. You probably were the one who killed G-mama!" Dee jumped up out the chair, raising her voice and waving her hand back and forth.

Big Rob was in shock and worried that Dee was going to get him kicked out. He had just dealt with the cops and he really wasn't about to go through that shit again. As Dee went on, though, Rob was getting more pissed.

"Bitch, shut the fuck up and sit the fuck down! You don't know what the fuck you're talking about. I ain't kill no muthafuckin' body and how the fuck you know she's pregnant?"

"Are you out your skull talking to me like that?" The boxer started coming out of her.

"Hell yea, Bitch! Your stupid ass, screaming that shit out loud up here and we fuck around and get me arrested again. That shit'll get you fucked up," Big Rob whispered while holding his anger and trying to calm Dee's voice down in the process.

"Fucked up like you did my girl G-mama, muthafucka? Huh?" Dee stood on her tiptoes and threw her finger in his face.

The nurses were changing over shifts and they all were looking in the room as the argument started to go down. A few were afraid to walk in, but one older nurse with silver hair and glasses on the tip of her nose decided she wasn't scared. She walked around the nurses' desk with her short and stout granny prance hands on her hips glaring dismay in her eyes.

Big Rob straightened up and took a few steps away. But Dee's emotions wouldn't let her ease up that easily. Before the nurse could open her mouth to tell them to keep it down or they would be asked to leave, Dee was already in full-blown emotions.

"This man is a murderer. It's his fault she's in here. Y'all need to call the police to get him the fuck outta here!" Dee pointed here finger and as she reached over Biggie's hospital bed.

Rob rubbed his hands over his face, trying to keep cool because he was ready to slap the fuck out of Dee, even if he had to deal with the cops again. He had been through enough. All he wanted to do was see Biggie and find out if she was going to be all right.

The nurse stood between the both of them. "Keep your voices down. There are people in here resting, trying to recover and if this is your friend, you should respect her enough to allow her to rest. I don't know you or this gentleman's situation, but I'm asking you both to leave now and don't return to this floor together. She's not having any more visitors today."

Dee could not believe this little old bitch had the nerve to throw her out. She grabbed her jacket and purse and looked the nurse in the face as if she would whip her ass and stormed out of the now silent hospital room. Big Rob stayed behind for a minute because he still had questions and somebody was going to answer them one way or another.

"Sir, I have asked you to leave." The old nurse stood there with her hands on her stout hips and slightly tapped her to small feet.

"Yea, you did, but I can't leave without some answers. That bitch told me that Biggie is pregnant. Is that true? Is she carrying my seed?" Big Rob asked with pleading eyes.

The nurse was not sure but for some reason she felt his sincerity. "I just came on my shift. Although I don't like your vulgar ways of expressing your emotions, I do see that you are very concerned. Let me get her file and I can give you more information after I do. I must ask you to please leave." The nurse walked out the room and around the nurses' station to find Biggie's chart.

As she conversed with the other nurses about what was going on, Rob sat on the side of Biggie's bed and rubbed her forehead with one hand while the other hand caressed the top of her hand. He did not know what to say. The feelings he had for Biggie were strong and they were real. Although he knew he was wrong for having them and that because of this, it was his fault she was in the hospital, he didn't regret his feelings for her. He suddenly wondered, *if that bitch Dee thought he was the one who murdered that gay bitch, maybe Biggie thought it too.*

Rob pulled away from Biggie. *She might wake up believing I'm the one who killed her home girl,* he thought to himself. Rob jumped up out the chair and stormed out the room with regret for allowing himself to feel soft for another bitch. With thoughts bursting through his mind and emotions flowing through his veins, he tried to get out of there as fast as he could.

"Sir, sir, wait. I have the information you asked for." The old nurse ran around the nurses with her stout legs looking like they were moving faster than she actually was.

It was too late. Big Rob was already out the security doors and headed into the elevator without looking back.

CHAPTER 4

Dee was furious. She couldn't believe she allowed that old ass, stubby fart of a nurse kick her out. She drove through every stop light before she realized what she was doing.

"Calm down, Dee. Calm down." She took a deep breath then blew out a long exhale. "I don't feel like going back to the house to deal with Peaches' ass. I need to go to the shop anyway. I can get a good cup of coffee and check the phones. I know all my clients going crazy." She spoke to herself as if she was speaking to another person. "What the fuck!" Dee blurted before she could gather the view in front of her.

Her shop had been trashed. Windows were busted out, the memorial that was set outside for G-mama was destroyed and from the fire department and police patrol cars that surrounded the strip, it seemed to have been set on fire. Dee sat in her car staring through her windshield in disbelief. Was she seeing what she thought she was seeing?

An employee of the neighboring coffee shop pointed Dee out to the police. "There's the owner right there, Ms. Dee. Ms. Dee they need to talk to you." The young punk rock white girl, with the punkie Brewster look waved for Dee to come to them.

But Dee could not move. She could feel her baby doing flips in her stomach and she began to get lightheaded. Her breathing was shallow and she felt the vomit filling up her esophagus. Everything seemed to be moving in slow motion. She turned her head to the driver side window where the fire department control officer was slowly trying to tell her something, but his mouth was moving too slow for her to understand or was her brain moving too slow to connect all the words?

"Ma'am? Open…the …door…sooo…weeeeeee…can…help…yyyoouuu!" Through the closed window, the officer sounded like a robot running out of battery juice. Dee's vision was blurry. *Am I having a stroke*, she thought to herself. Dee rubbed her belly for comfort, afraid to open the door and afraid to not open the door all at the same time. Dee reached for her purse to get her phone and call Jeremiah. She needed someone to help her. Before she could dial the number, the fireman had already opened her door.

"Ma'am, are you the owner of this establishment?" said the 6'4" caramel complexion fireman with a sexy, deep voice while he reached his big hands in to help Dee out of the car.

"Yes," Dee whispered as she took hold of the officer's hand with her left hand while holding her phone in the right.

"I'm sorry this happened to you," the officer began. "This must be a lot to take in, especially in your condition, but it looks like a case of arson. The CPD said they have been trying to get in touch with you all morning. Is that your phone?"

Dee looked at her shop, then to the police officers standing around and back to the hottie fireman. Finally, she looked down at her phone, feeling weaker by the minute. She sighed. "Yes," she admitted without an explanation.

Tears began to roll down Dee's face. This fireman had no idea what she been through over the last few weeks and now this. He could see she was not doing well, so he scooped her up in his muscular arms and carried her over to the ambulance so the EMS could examine her. What Dee did not realize was her phone had indeed called Jeremiah and he heard what the fireman was saying to her. He could hear over the phone that the fireman was making passes at Dee. Since he was less than two miles checking in on a client, he decided to rush over to her. But what he saw when he arrived sent fury through his bones.

"Now this motherfucker playing Superman?" Jeremiah said in an angry, heavy voice.

The fireman couldn't control his impulses. He gently brushed Dee's hair from her face as he stared in her face like he was trying to memorize her to draw or paint her. Dee began to feel uneasy. She blushed, even in her time of distress. There was something about him that intrigued her. Just as their eyes connected, the moment was immediately interrupted by Jeremiah's aggressive, what-the-fuck approach.

"Don't you have a job to do, dude?" Jeremiah questioned with pure attitude.

"Jeremiah!" Dee cried out as if she knew he would be coming. "Baby, I'm so happy to see you. Why is this happening to me?" She pointed toward her shop.

The fireman gathered his self, but continued to congest Dee's space.
Jeremiah noticed the fireman wasn't moving. "You can go on with what you need to take care of. Her man is here now. I'm sure if you have any questions for her you would

need to do some work first to be able to do so." Jeremiah shot the fireman a look that said "step off."

The fireman shot an evil eye right back at Jeremiah. "My job is to make sure this beautiful mom-to-be is safe and coherent to understand what is going on. And if I have to take her up in my arms to do so, I'm only doing what is required of me. It's not always pretty, but there are times when I enjoy it more than others. This just happens to be one of those times. Sad it had to be under these conditions." He winked his eye at Dee and walked away.

Dee closed her eyes and began to rub her stomach in disbelief. *Are these two serious? My shop has been destroyed and they're having a testosterone contest.* She also knew that Jeremiah did not care about to much of anything when he felt challenged, but this fireman should know better.

"One of your boyfriends, huh?" Jeremiah questioned.

"Wha, WHAT? Really? Is that what concerns you? My shop is a disaster, my friend is dead, my other friend is laid up in a hospital bed and your biggest concern is a muthafuckin' fireman I've never seen before in my life, and if I fucked him?" Dee cried out in breathless words.

The EMS drivers began to walk away, trying to give them privacy. Everyone was standing around watching all the commotion already, but somehow it became more interesting when Dee's pregnant body jumped down out of the ambulance and took it to Jeremiah. She staggered around as if she was under the influence. She screamed and yelled, which made Jeremiah furious. He hated to be confronted in such a manner, especially by a woman. The fireman saw what was going on and he walked over. He cleared his throat and said, "Is everything all right over here? Excuse me, sir. This woman is with child and should not be going through anything extra right now. If you keep it up, I'm going to ask you to leave the premises."

"You're going to ask me to leave the premises? Motherfucker, do you know who I am?" Jeremiah cocked his head to the side like a crazy man.

"No." The fireman smirked as if he wasn't impressed.

"Look, you need to go on 'bout your business and leave me and my pregnant fiancé to handle our business before I file a federal complaint against you and your whole department that will relieve of your duties, and get your ass fined with so many harassment citations you will be paying out your ass." Jeremiah used his lawyer talk to put the fireman in his place.

Unfazed, the fireman stepped in and so did Jeremiah.

Dee stepped in between both of them. She put her hands up and pleaded with them to stop. The police finally intervened after Dee had already approached the situation, which pissed her off. *It took them long enough,* Dee thought to herself. It was as if they wanted to see them fight.

One officer pulled Dee to the side asking if she wanted them to ask Jeremiah to leave. They told her if she did not want to answer, blink twice and they would escort him to his car. Lawyer or not, they would not be having him cause any more excitement. As she thought to herself, she could see the fireman looking over in her direction again. The chief was scolding him for losing his cool, but what the chief said seemed to be going in one ear and out the other. He was imprinting on Dee right before her own eyes and she was allowing it.

"Ma'am, ma'am, are you okay?" the police officer called to Dee.

She took a deep breath as she was driven from the deep stare she and the fireman shared. "Um no, no, he's fine." She was not about to cross Jeremiah, knowing he would make it hard for her to focus on the matter at hand, and the fireman.

Jeremiah paced back and forth like a dog in rage watching the sexy fireman as he led Dee to her torched beauty salon, showing her where the fire began. He let her salvage some of the things that could be used, although they had smoke damage. He held Dee's arm and looked in her face as he directed her further into the shop. This only made Jeremiah see red. He tried to bum rush his way through, but the police officers would not let him anywhere near Dee.

"Excuse me, I'm her attorney. She needs me for insurance purposes." Jeremiah tried to use his profession to get his way.

"Well, I'm sure when she gets to that part they'll call you. Besides, she seems to be in good hands," one officer teased as he scarfed down a donut from the coffee shop next door.

Jeremiah yelled to Dee. "Baby, tell these officers you need your lawyer for insurance purposes."

Dee was so annoyed by Jeremiah she did not know what came over her. With all that she was going through, how could he act like it was all about him. Then she thought to herself how she was truly infatuated with the fireman and the feeling was mutual. She could feel it. Jeremiah could see it, and so could everyone else. This made Jeremiah very angry. He tried to control his anger because he did not want to lose Dee and his baby, but he was ready to put hands on somebody.

He had a flashback of slapping Dee and seeing the hurt in her eyes. He could not bear to see that look on her face again.

Come on, Jeremiah, get yourself together. This will be over soon and you can take Dee home and help her get through all the shit she's going through. But before I do that, let me make a few calls and find out about Mr. Fireman. What was his name again? Jeremiah began to call in some favors.

Dee didn't understand what came over her. Not even five hours ago, she was bumping and grinding with Jeremiah. Now she was having lustful feelings for a fireman she didn't even know. And with all that was going on, she needed to be thinking of how she was going to take care of her clients. Who was she going to hire to take the girls' places to service their clients, and where was going to put them to do so? So many thoughts went through her mind. With the smell of the smoke and dead water, she needed to excuse herself.

"I'm sorry. Can we do this another time? I really need to go lie down and take all this in." She waved her hand as if she was in church testifying.

Dee gave the police officer and the fireman her card and walked out. Jeremiah cuffed her arm as soon as she stepped outside and gave the fireman face as he helped Dee to her car.

"Baby, I'm going to follow you home, okay?" Jeremiah kissed Dee on the cheek as he hooked her into the seatbelt."

"No, baby, please go take care of your business I just want to go home, check on Peaches, take a nice shower, rest up and go back to the hospital to check on Biggie." Dee leaned her head to the side to reassure him she would be fine.

Jeremiah closed Dee's door and walked away, after rubbing her pregnant belly.

CHAPTER 5

Dee stumbled in the door, drained with exhaustion, and dropped her keys on the table in the foyer. Her purse fell to the floor as she bumped the tall table that sat in the middle of the foyer with a big bowl of real oranges.

"Peaches, I'm home. Peaches, where are you? I need you. Please. The shop…" Dee stopped in her tracks as she walked by the sitting room. She took three big steps backwards to look in and things were in a disarray. *Wait, my door wasn't locked. It wasn't even closed.* "Oh shit! Peaches! Peaches, I know you're not on one. Come here now!"

Dee started to get scared. She ran to her purse, grabbed her cell phone out of it and noticed she had an abundance of voicemails and calls from a number she didn't recognize. She pressed 1 on her phone to retrieve her messages.

"Dee, this is Peaches. I'm in jail. G-mama came in and called my phone and I hit a cop and possibly killed two people and I know you're with that back stabbing bitch, but COME GET ME! Dee, help me!"

In the background Dee heard someone say, "Ma'am, ma'am please hang up the phone."

She proceeded to the next message. "Hi I'm detective Maxwell and I'm calling on behalf of…" then the phone went blank. "Please give me a call at 216-555-1234…" It went blank again. "…at the fifth distinct…" The phone went blank again.

"What the fuck!" Dee jumped up, ran upstairs, jumped in the shower, and quickly changed her clothes. As she pulled on her maternity jeans and college sweatshirt she dialed back the number Detective Maxwell left to see if she could contact someone on the raggedy phone system.

"Hi, yes, you called me. My name is Dee," she began, then gave her full government name. Dee rolled her eyes as she went on with her conversation. "I'm looking for my friend..."

"Yes, we have your friend. She says you can explain why she has been drinking and something about speaking to the dead. Ma'am, do you know what kind of drugs your friend may have taken?"

"What?" Dee began, offended at the officer's suggestion that Peaches would be on drugs. "As far as I know, she doesn't take any drugs. What you need to understand officer..."

Detective Maxwell cut Dee off again. "No, ma'am. What *you* need to understand is that your friend has committed some serious crimes and if you and she do not co-operate with us, we can't help her. We need you to come down to the station so we can ask you a few questions. Are you available now?"

Dee took a deep breath, trying to conduct herself in a professional manner. "Yes, sir, I am available. Please give me the information so I can be on my way."

Dee wrote down the precinct information on the notepad she kept on the corner table. She hung up the phone and placed it close to her heart, leaned back against the wall and took a deep breath and slowly exhaled. She thought to herself, when *is it going to stop? What have I done so wrong to be getting this horrible test?* She shook her head to stop the negative thoughts. She felt herself asking the same questions she had been asking since all the drama began. It was time for answers. She grabbed her purse, keys and walked out the door.

When Dee got in the car, she put the key in the ignition, put on her seatbelt, turned on her radio and checked her mirrors, all in full detail, which was something she never usually did. But with all the craziness going on, she felt this would be a good look for now on.

Dee slowly pulled out her driveway and headed toward the police station. She tried not to let her mind drift off into any of the fuckery that was already going on. She was too afraid of losing focus and causing more chaos, so she tilted her head back and forth to release the stress in her neck as she listened to slow grooves playing on 93.1. When she reached the police station she was stopped in the parking lot by officers sitting in their cars, facing opposite directions conversing like it was part of their job description, not paying any attention to her trying to park. It wasn't that they didn't see her; they just wanted to finish their conversation. Dee rolled her eyes and honked her horn. Both police officers checked their mirrors and continued in their conversation. Dee blew again. The male officer opened his car door, walked up to Dee's window and asked for her license and registration.

Dee's eyes widened. "Are you fucking kidding me? You block the driveway and act as if you don't see me while you're flirting or whatever the fuck you doing, and after I blow my horn to make sure you see me, you have the nerve to want to run my name? Where the fuck was you when my friend was getting killed, or when I was getting my ass beat, or when my friend was beating the shit out of my other friend for sleeping with her husband, or when my fucking shop burned down? WHERE WERE YOU THEN OFFICER UM UMM..." Dee looked for his name on his shirt and rubbed her belly. The baby was making her feel nauseated. The officer didn't say another word. He walked back to his vehicle, got in and moved out of her way. The female officer looked over at him.

"I think you did the right thing. She looked like a woman on edge and I know that's the look I have when I'm 'bout to lose it."

Dee pulled into a parking space, put her hands over her face, took another deep breath and burst into tears. She could not take it. She allowed herself to cry for five minutes, pulled down her mirror to check her face, fixed her makeup and then opened the truck door to walk into the police station. But, of course, at that time morning sickness kicked in and Dee had to run over to the garbage can right outside the door to vomit what seemed like her entire insides.

A female sergeant with long burnt orange dreads pinned up into a nice up do, with soft brown eyes and thick curves that fit her uniform nice and comfortably walked out the door. She stood about 5' 9" and had a soft, but stern voice. She walked over to Dee to see if she needed any help. The sergeant immediately recognized Dee from her salon.

"Dee, right?" the sergeant asked.

Dee looked up with a weakened stare. "Yes, uumm, please excuse me," she said as she wiped her mouth with the napkin the sergeant was handing her. Dee didn't recognize her. "Do I know you?"

"Yes, I came to your shop in a hurry one day. I was in a wedding and needed my dreads twisted and pinned up…"

"Oh and colored." Dee blurted out, remembering the day so well. It was a day G-mama turned up the music in the shop and dragged Dee in the middle of the floor to dance. The Temptations' song My Girl was playing and they all started singing, dancing laughing. The whole shop joined in. Dee's eyes started to fill up with tears. "You said you were trying to meet some of the men at the wedding and you needed to cover up your gray, on your head and down below." Dee tried to get her composure, but the tears were steadily rolling down her face.

"Yes," the officer chuckled. "You do remember, but you don't have to cry about it." The sergeant handed Dee more napkins. "I remember we were singing and dancing and I thought it was the best experience I have ever had in a shop. You guys moved fast and didn't have me in there all day. What's wrong, honey? You seem to have a lot going on?"

"Yes, I do, but I have to get inside. I'm late for an appointment, but thank you so much for your help." Dee did not want to get into it all, so she gathered herself and focused on the situation at hand.

"Okay, I understand. Sometimes we as woman have to release one way or another, but if you ever need to talk, please give me a call. The sergeant handed Dee her card. "Actually, please call me. I really loved your work and I need another appointment."

Dee didn't want to tell her about the shop, so she took the card and said, "I promise." The ladies went their separate ways.

Once Dee hit the front desk, she could not remember the name of the detective who called her. The officer at the desk looked down from a tall oak desk that was filled with flyers. He was an overweight white man, bald on the top with gray sides and bifocals that hung from the tip of his nose. His blues eyes peeked from over the glasses and his potbelly looked as if it wanted to pop through his buttons. "May I help you, ma'am?" the officer asked as he glared at Dee over his bifocals.

"Yes, I have an appointment with a detective, but I can't remember his name.

"Okay, then I can't help you." The officer sat back in his seat and folded his arms on top of his belly.

Dee rolled her eyes, thinking to herself, *I know, muthafucka. That's why I have my phone in my hand so I can't look it up.* She looked in her phone, found the number, and instantly remembered. "Maxwell. Detective Maxwell," she said with a little attitude in her voice to let the officer know he pissed her off.

He lifted his eyebrow, picked up the phone, whispered something under his voice and hung up the phone. "Have a seat over there. Someone will be with you in a moment." The officer pointed to a bench across the walkway. Dee smiled politely, gathered her phone and some flyers off the tall desk and turned to walk toward the bench. "Have a nice day," she said in a sarcastic voice.

"You too," the officer said back in the same tone.

As Dee sat and waited for someone to come and speak with her, she began to rub her belly and drift off into thought. She recalled all that had happened in her life in the last few weeks. She started to get worked up again when a young rookie walked up to her and said the detective would see her now.

She followed him down a hallway toward a pair of double doors where she had to place her hand on an activation pad to enter through. Once they were through the double doors, Dee had to place her purse on top of a table where a fully armed officer searched it thoroughly. After the search of her bag the officer used a metal detecting wand over her as she held her arms out like an airplane and turned very slowly. As Dee was turning she felt this sudden heat all over her body, like someone was watching her. It was more intense than an unknown or casual stare. When she reached around back to the officer and his wand, Detective Maxwell was walking up to her with a familiar face and body.

"Wow, it's you," the fireman whispered.

Dee looked around in a state of embarrassment for no reason at all. "Yes, it's me." She blushed.

Det. Maxwell watch both of them stare at each other for what seemed like forever then extended his hand and said," Hi, I'm Det. Darién Maxwell and this is my little brother Christophe Maxwell. I take it you two have met before?"

"Christophe the fireman?" Dee blurted with a breathless exhale and a smirk.

"Yes, yes we have met. This is the young lady that I told you about with the shop that caught on fire, Max." Christophe said with a smile.

Dee shook off her now sensual stare with Christophe and focused her eyes on Det. Maxwell. "I'm here about my friend. Can you please let me see her and tell me in full detail what's going on?"

"You may want to sit down before we let you see her. Your friend is in some real trouble. The thing is, I believe she already has some issues she is dealing with and I need you to fill me in on what is going on before I can offer her help. She's been raving on about a G-mama?" Det. Maxwell said G's name with a question, hoping Dee would jump in and give some insight on that. When she remained silent, he continued. "She was talking as if this person was in the room with her. She's also discussed how she attacked someone and she might be a killer." Tears started to roll down Dee's face, but she still did not say a word. Det. Maxwell continued. "Your friend caused an accident that has killed two people and ran into my car." Dee gasped after hearing that information. The detective paused, offered Dee some tissues, and tilted his head for permission to continue. "When we arrested her, she was hysterical, and for lack of a better word wacked out. Now, I would've assumed she was on drugs, but she seemed too afraid to be a drug addict. However, she did reek of alcohol. Now I see that some of the information I have shared with you has shaken you in a way that leads me to believe you know exactly what is going on with your friend. What I need you to do is make me understand it."

As Dee adjusted her body to figure out where she would begin, Det. Maxwell's assistant walked over to him and gave him a folder and a note. He read the note, looked up over his desk, waved his hand, and gave a head nod to his brother who was seated at another detective's desk with his hand over his mouth and sadness on his face.

Det. Maxwell focused his attention back on Dee as she tried to gather her composure, but could not find a way to hold on to it. She just started talking. "I was in a relationship with a man that was beating me up, and G-mama was sleeping with Peaches. We didn't know Big Rob found out and beat up Peaches and kicked her out. Biggie started fucking Big Rob, somebody killed G-mama and she was the sweetest person you'll ever want to meet. We don't' know who did it. Jeremiah was so mad at her, but Big Rob was too."

Det. Maxwell tried to keep up and write everything down as Dee was rambling on. His eyes darted from the paper to Dee in disbelief of the story he was hearing, but he did not interrupt her. He needed to get it all down and she seemed to be on a roll.

Dee continued. "Peaches beat up on Biggie when she found out about her and Big Rob. Biggie's in the hospital sedated and she's pregnant, but she doesn't know my shop burned down and everything is going wrong." Dee broke out into a full merciful cry. "Now this. Why is all this happening?" she screamed out so loud the whole precinct stopped and turned toward Det. Maxwell's desk.

Christophe jumped up over a chair and around to his brother's desk, and wrapped his arms around Dee. Det. Maxwell looked at his brother and knew there was something brewing and that was not a good thing, especially since Dee had so much going on and was apparently carrying the baby of a woman beater.

Dee buried her head in Christophe's chest and balled her eyes out. The tighter he held her, the more she cuddled into his arms and she felt safe there. He leaned his head down on top of her and slowly rocked her back and forth.

"Max, why don't you get her some water?" Christophe nodded his head toward the water cooler to get his brother to stop giving him that I-don't-approve look.

Det. Maxwell mumbled under his breath. "This dude giving me orders like he work here. This my damn office. Falling for this woman. I know it and now I have to be the monster, whatever, whatever." He took a deep breath while he filled the clear cup with water and smiled at the other detectives who were passing by.

As he walked back to his desk, he noticed that his rookie assistant was standing at her desk with a tissue crying, and far past her, his chief was peeking out from the alabaster horizontal blinds with evil lurking eyes that shook his bowels. He knew that meant trouble.

He reached his desk where Christophe was still calming Dee. Max handed her the water and looked his brother in the eyes with a stare that said, "Follow me now." Christophe knew his brother well and obliged all while looking confused and wondering what was wrong. Just as Max was about to tear into his little brother's ass, his chief screamed out her glass office door.

"Maxwell! My office, now!" The 5'6'' 115 lb woman with fair skin and long brown hair paced back and forth with one hand on her hip.

Max pointed his finger at his brother and opened his mouth to say something, then pressed his lips together tight. He shook his finger and then his head and walked away.

He headed down the aisle to the chief's office, walked in and closed the door behind him "Yes sir?" He stood in front of the chief's desk and addressed her as she liked to be addressed.

The chief walked behind her desk, placed both hands on top of the files on her desk and stared up to Max directly in his eyes. "Does this look like a trauma center to you, or a drama hall, maybe a circus?"

"No, sir!" Max stayed at attention. He had been on the chief's bad side ever since she transferred there and he really did not want the problems.

"Well, why do you have a pregnant woman screaming around in my precinct, a brother leaping over my furniture like Link Hayes from the Mob Squad, and all my detectives in an uproar? Which, by the way, if your brother is a fireman why is he always in my precinct, anyway?" As the chief went on, she began to pace around her desk again.

"With all due respect, sir, the young lady is a friend to the woman that caused the accident today, and she just found out her friend is be charged with vehicular homicide and she's…"

"I don't care. This is a police station, and not a day care. Get it together, Maxwell. Don't forget to close my door." The chief sat at her desk looking at paperwork, not giving Maxwell anymore thought.

The detective walked out, slammed the door and aggressively walked to his desk. He snatched his little brother by the arm. "Yo, what's up with you and this girl?" Max stared Christophe in the face showing he was not in the mood for BS. He had just had his ass handed to him by the chief. He had to get Dee in to see her friend and find out what the hell was going on with their situation, so he needed to know his brother was cool, because Dee might be going down with her friend.

Christophe said, "Bruh, I don't know, for real. Since I met her, I have had this deep connection to her that I can't explain and I feel like she has the same feelings for me. You know the feeling like you've met someone before, although you have never crossed paths?"

"Well, she might be tied up within this case somehow and I don't need you compromising it. Plus, Chief is really having a fit with you being here all the time, so bruh you gotta go."

"WHAT!" Christophe's eyes bucked in disbelief. "Bruh?" He threw his hands up as if to say, what's up? Don't do this to me.

Max pointed his finger toward the door and put his head down without words.

Christophe turned toward Dee. "Nice to see you again. I hope all is well. Make sure you get a good lawyer."

As soon as Dee heard lawyer she remembered Jeremiah. She searched the room to see if he was there, and fear entered her stomach like a bolt of lightning. She should have called him to begin with. *He's going to want to know why I didn't call and if I call him now and he sees Christophe down here it's going to be trouble. I can't with this right now. I have to find out what's going on with Peaches before I do anything, I'll call him after*, she thought to herself as she waved bye to Christophe. She really wished he could stay. Something about him made her feel safe and comfortable.

Max walked back over to his desk. "Okay, I'm going to take you down to see your friend, but first I want you to do me a favor. If you know of any reason, or you see anything different than what's normal, you be honest with me and let me know, okay?"
Dee nodded in agreement, wondering in her mind what Peaches was doing to make them seriously question her mental stability.

Once they left Max's desk Dee followed him down a long hallway. Max swiped his badge and they entered a set of double doors where a female officer sat with blonde hair, blue eyes, and a hard face. She appeared to have her hand under the desk as if she was holding onto a strap under there, other than the gun on her hip.

Max greeted her with a head nod.

The officer smiled, nodded back, and said. "Detective."

Dee just stayed behind Max, figuring it did not matter if she spoke or not. They turned down another away which led to another door and a staircase.
Detective Maxwell turned to Dee, which made her bump into him because she had a million things running through mind and didn't realize he was stopping.

"Are you okay to take the stairs? If not, we can use the elevators. I'm just used to taking the stairs, good way to keep in shape," he said as he patted his what appeared to be a six pack.

Dee nodded again, too afraid to open her mouth and bring the rain of tears she was fighting so hard to keep back.

It was two floors down, six flights of stairs. Dee thought to herself, *I should've said elevators*. They reached another security door. This time Max had to pick up the phone and speak to someone. The door clicked and slid open, where another door stood. Max put in a code and a bright light waved over him. An officer spoke from behind the glass window, "State your name and your badge number."

Before Dee knew it, she whispered under her breath, "What is this? Men in Black?"

Max looked over his shoulder. "What was that?"

Dee shook her head as if she hadn't said a word.

Max smiled to himself as he played her words back in his mind, putting them together. It was funny.

After they were allowed through the security door, the officer walked around and asked Dee to hold up her arms as she walked through the metal detector. Once she moved through there they used the wand for extra security, then asked her to remove her shoes. She wiggled her toes and shook out her hair.

"Really, is all of this necessary?" Dee rolled her eyes at the officer as she put her shoes back on.

The officer replied in deep tone for a woman, "Very. You'd be surprised what we find on people, and where we find it. We have to make sure we take all precautions for our safety and the inmates' safety as well."

"Well, hell, I just found out she was being held in jail a few hours ago. Doesn't give me much time to plan anything."

Max replied, "That is an indication you might not be criminal material, because a criminal can come up with a plan in a matter of seconds if they really want to get something done."

The officer shook her head in agreement with Max.

Dee replied. "Um, so can a woman. However, it doesn't make her any more criminal than you."

The officer raised her eyebrow and shook her head in agreement with Dee.

Max looked back in forth between both the women and decided to keep his mouth closed. He realized he was outnumbered and anything he said would be used against him as a man.

Once they entered through the next hallway, they reached a door on the right side of the hallway. Max stopped, opened the door, waved his hand for Dee to enter first, and he entered behind her. He turned to her, gave her a look, sat on the desk in the room, and took a deep breath.

"Now, if you are sure you know your friend then what you see might shake you up a little. She does not know you are here so please don't stir up too much emotion or make any sudden outbursts. Like I said, I need you to tell me the truth so I can help her, okay?" Max lifted his eyebrow to show Dee he was serious.

Dee nodded her head up and down without speaking any words. She was too nervous to speak, not knowing what to expect.

Max turned on a switch, which illuminated a window to another room. He then tapped a switch on the desk that read LISTEN. Dee wondered what all this was for, where Peaches was, and what was in this white room. All of a sudden, Peaches jumped up out of nowhere threw herself into the mirror and looked out into space. This startled Dee and Max. Peaches took a deep breath, slid herself from the mirror and walked into the middle of the white room and sat on the floor facing her back toward the mirror. Peaches peeked over her left shoulder with a blank glare.

"Dee, I know you're there," Peaches whispered in a light voice.

Dee's eyes widened as she took a deep breath.

Max looked at the expression on Dee's face. She was filled with overwhelming fear.

"I thought you said no one told her I was here?" Dee lashed out to Max.

Max pushed the listen button. "We didn't. I don't know how she knew you were here. Honestly." Max pushed the listen button again. He held up his index finger to Dee and listened in.

"Don't be surprised. G-mama told me you would come. I didn't believe her, though. You were never there for me."

She used her right hand to turn herself around and look directly at the mirror as if she could look right into Dee's eyes.

"But here you are. G, I guess I owe you one."
Peaches laughed and looked over to her right side as if G-mama was really sitting right next to her.

Dee sat straight up and did not say a word. Tears rolled down her face. Seeing her friend in this state and for her to believe she was talking to G-mama was heartbreaking. Dee wanted to believe it too. She wanted to tell G how sorry she was and how she wished things could be different. But she had to come back to her right mind and help Peaches to get out of there.

"Dee, how could you? How could you dog G-mama like that and let them get her? You knew how much she cared for you, how much she loved you. How!" Peaches banged on the mirror.

Dee jumped and began to bawl. Although Max was looking right at Peaches he jumped too.

"I'm sorry," Dee said through tears and her running nose."

But Peaches could not hear her.

"You know the worst part about it? You did it for a no good, crazy ass man. You're just like your mama. Fucked-up bitch that will do anything for some dick. Get your ass beat, watch your friend die. Hell, you would probably let him kill me too!" Peaches snarled her face in disgust.

"Stop, stop it! I'm not my mother. I didn't mean it. I didn't mean for G to die."
Dee jumped up and ran out the room into the hallway where she fell to her knees.

Detectives and officers stopped and looked. Max was stunned by what he was hearing and some of what he saw.

"Please let me help your friend. She needs some full medical attention. This will help me keep her out of prison and in a mental facility so she can't harm herself or others." Max extended his hand to help Dee up off the floor.

Crying, Dee managed to muster. "Thank you."

"You're welcome. I can't promise anything but after seeing this, I can't imagine anyone trying to convict her of a crime." Max felt sorry for Dee.

He escorted her to the exit after having her fill out paperwork to help get Peaches' information together and told her he would be in touch. As Dee stepped outside the police department, she noticed Christophe standing by his dodge F250. She didn't know if he was waiting for her, so she walked by him still in tears and not really feeling like being bothered.

"Hi," Christophe said as he walked toward to her.

Dee didn't respond with words. She just waved good-bye.

"I was waiting for you. Are you okay?" He reached out to open her car door.

Dee sniffed. "Why, why are you waiting for me?"

"I don't know. Something in me would not let me leave. I know this sounds crazy and this is not a pick-up line or anything like that, but I'm drawn to you somehow and I can't fight it, and to be honest, I don't want to. Look, it seems like you've been through a lot and I'm not asking for anything, but I would like to be here for you if you would allow it," Christophe said as he handed Dee a hanky.

Dee felt offended. "What? You don't even know me, and unless you're blind, I'm pregnant by a man you met me with earlier. Also, I have all this craziness around me. What's wrong with you? Are you some type of crazy ass mofo that comes on to women when they're vulnerable so that you can misuse them?"

Christophe was lost for words. It was not his intention to make her feel this way. He honestly could not explain the feelings he was experiencing for Dee and he thought the honest approach was the best. But now he was second-guessing his decision. Christophe looked around and tried to decide what his next move would be, but he had nothing.

He smiled to himself. "Look, you've been through a lot today. I'm sure you must be hungry and you have to feed your little one. Can I please take you somewhere to get something to eat?"

Dee questioned his smile. She stepped back on one leg, and looked around to see if enough people were around so if she screamed someone would come to help her. But when she looked into his eyes there was something there that felt warm and inviting.

Dee rubbed her belly and said, "Come to think of it, I'm starving. Although I don't feel much like eating."

"I can understand that. Most times when someone has been through as much as you, either they overeat or never eat. In your case, you are eating for two and if you don't eat, your baby doesn't. Look, I have the perfect place, even if you don't decide to eat anything. It's a nice place to relax your mind. Just follow me. It's not far from here," Christophe said as he helped Dee into her car.

When they pulled up to the restaurant Dee realized it was her favorite place. She began to cry as it was also the last place her, G-mama and Biggie were all at together.

Christophe stood outside Dee's car door lightly tapping on her window. "Hey, what's going on in there? Are you okay?"

Dee looked up and tried to wipe away her tears. "This is my favorite place. My girls and I were here a few weeks ago." Dee shook her head, crying more tears.

Christophe saw the sadness in her eyes. "Look, I'm so sorry. I didn't know. This is my favorite place too. When I'm off I come here to gather myself. I thought it would be good for you. Please forgive me."

Dee got out the car. "Thank you and don't apologize. You didn't know.

They both walked toward the restaurant and just as they walked in, who's sitting at a table right in front, in what looked like a very important business dinner? He caught her eyes.

"Jeremiah," Dee whispered under her breath.

The look in Jeremiah's eyes was murder, murder, murder. Dee could feel the anger shooting through her body. When Christophe tried to lead her to a table, her legs could not move. Her feet were stuck to the floor as if they were nailed there.

Christophe rubbed her shoulders, not noticing what was happening. "Are you okay? Is it too much for you or something?"

Dee took her eyes off Jeremiah, turned to Christophe and took a deep breath. "It's him. He's really mad."

Christophe looked over the room and saw the anger cut him from across the room. "Oh, your boyfriend is here. Let's go say hi."

"No, no, no. You don't know him. He's very…"

Christophe pulled Dee around. "Is he putting his hands on you?"

Before Dee could answer, Jeremiah was up on both of them. "What's going on here, Dee?"

"Nothing. How are you? I believe we met earlier today." Christophe extended his hand again to Jeremiah.

And again Jeremiah ignored the gesture and refused to shake his hand. "Dee, I asked you a question." Jeremiah spoke to Dee, never taking his eyes off of Christophe.

Dee was shaking with fear. She didn't want Jeremiah to hurt her again nor did she want him to hurt Christophe.

Jeremiah leaned in kissed her on the cheek with his eyes still on Christophe. He whispered in Dee's ear. "I'm not going to deal with this now, because I'm in a business meeting and I don't want to fuck this motherfucker up in here, but we will talk about this later. Do you understand?"

Dee shook her head, turned around and walked out of the restaurant. Christophe didn't know what Jeremiah said to her, but he didn't like it. Christophe stood there staring at Jeremiah for what seemed like hours with Jeremiah staring right back at him. Jeremiah's dinner companions stared to see what the situation was about, but it was over before it started. Christophe turned his back to chase after Dee.

"Dee, Dee, please wait." Christophe grabbed Dee's car door.

"Look I shouldn't have been here with you anyway. You don't understand. I have a lot going on and he, he's a very powerful man. I need to get to the hospital anyway. Thanks for your kindness, but I really need to go." Dee grabbed her car door and pulled off.

"She's so beautiful. Why is she wrapped up in this dude? I should just leave it alone, but I don't want to." Christophe spoke to himself.

Back inside the restaurant one of Jeremiah's business associates asked, "Is everything all right?"

"Oh yes, just a couple I represented in case. They still owe money. I told them it wasn't a good look to be having dinner when they haven't paid me in full." Jeremiah laughed out loud as if the situation was beneath him.

All his companions joined in on the laugh.

CHAPTER 6

"Dee, how long you been here." Biggie's groggy voice shook Dee as she slept in a chair beside her.

"Biggie, you're awake," Dee whispered, afraid to speak too loud.

A nurse walked in. "Hello, oh my gosh I'm so happy you're awake. I need to check your vitals so we can make sure your little one is all right."

Biggie removed the oxygen mask and said in a groggy whisper, "Little what?"

The nurse looked back at Dee and then at Biggie. "Baby, your baby. I'm sorry, I thought you knew that you were with child?"

Biggie exhaled so deeply her machine began to beep. Tears ran down the side of her face and she couldn't gain a breath. Dee gave her a sip of water. The nurse adjusted her bed and checked her vitals, trying to get her to calm down.

I thought that the father just didn't know. Well I figured he was the father because when he was here the other day and I mentioned to him that you were pregnant he looked like a deer caught in headlights and ran out of here. Oh dear, me and my big mouth."

"Big Rob was here?" Biggie looked at Dee for confirmation

Dee whispered. "I don't know."

"Okay, sweetie, I know this is a lot for you just waking up and all, but I need to get you all checked out and we need to run a few tests.

"Okay, but Dee stays. I don't want to be without you again. You can't leave me." Biggie reached out for Dee's hand.

Dee grabbed Biggie's hand. "I promise. I'm not going anywhere."

The nurse began to run her tests and asked Biggie a few questions. Two other nurses came in and out as well as the doctor who brought a few residents with him as he examined a few of his patients. Dee tried her best to stay out the way. She happed to glance toward the door and noticed her nightmare in the hallway.

Dee walked to the door.

"Dee, where you going?" Biggie looked over the doctor's shoulder to see her walking away.

Dee held up her hand, not wanting to overwhelm her friend.

"Jeremiah, look, this isn't a good time. I know you're upset about what happened at the restaurant, but it's not what you think."

"You have no idea what I think. What I know is my fiancé, my soon to be child's mother was at her favorite restaurant with a fireman that was hitting on her right in front of me not even twelve hours ago."

Dee took a deep breath and started to walk back to the room. "Yes, it looks bad, and I will give you all the information you want to know, but Biggie just woke up and I need to be in…"

Jeremiah grabbed her arm, cutting her off. "I don't give a fuck! You need to be explaining to me what the fuck you were doing there with him right now."

The nurses at the front desk all looked up to see what was going on.

Dee stared back at them. She wanted to scream at the pain he caused to her arm, but still didn't want to cause any commotion.

She rubbed his hand that held the tight grip on her arm. "You're right. You're right. When I got home, I found out that Peaches was in jail. I went to police station to find out what happened. It turns out she had a car accident and two people died. The detective on the case was his brother he was there when the detective questioned me and that is how we ended up seeing each other again. There, is that explanation enough?" Dee spoke through clenched teeth.

"You allowed yourself to be questioned without me? I'm a lawyer. Damn it, Dee, you could've said the wrong thing." Jeremiah grabbed his forehead.

"Don't speak to me like I'm stupid. I was there for my friend. After all I've been through in these last few weeks, the last thing I need is your jealous ass hanging over my shoulder."

Jeremiah grabbed her arm again.

"Go ahead. What'cha gonna do? Hit me? Push me down? Go ahead. I don't care anymore. You don't own me because I'm carrying your baby and wearing this stupid ass ring. And I still don't know if you killed my girl, my family." Dee removed the ring from her finger and threw it at him.

The youngest nurse at the desk jumped up. "Excuse me, we can't allow this. You both need to leave."

An older nurse with burnt orange dyed hair walked up. "Sir, you need to leave. Ma'am, your sister needs you."

Dee allowed the nurse to lead her back into Biggie's room. She was grateful the nurse came in when she did and saved her. She was also glad the nurse didn't cause too much drama to bring Biggie's attention to what was going on. She knew if that happened it would add more stress to biggie and she would want to get involved.

When she reached Biggie's bedside, Biggie was withdrawn and focused in a deep blank stare as if she was trying to recapture a moment but had too many visions going through her mind.

"Biggie, sweetie, are you okay?" Dee asked her friend surrounded by nurses and residents.

Biggie came back to focus. "Dee, I feel like I have something to tell you, but I can't bring myself to figure out what it is."

"It's okay, sweetie. Please don't stress yourself. You've been through a lot. Maybe it's all the drama you're thinking of and it seems as so." Dee knew what Biggie spoke of, but didn't want to bring too much back to memory to stress the baby.

"I don't care about stress, damn it. I know I need to tell you something. Stop treating me like a mental patient. I have been unconscious for what seems like a lifetime to wake up and find myself beaten and pregnant by my coworker's husband. I can't remember much of anything and these damn doctors and nurses are getting on my fucking nerves!" Biggie screamed to the top of her lungs.

"I'm sorry, I just want you to rest and get better. I need you right now. So much is going on. I'm scared and lost. Plus, your baby needs you to get better so that it can have a mommy to develop properly." Dee broke out in tears.

The nurses all looked at one another. They were finished with everything and wanted to give the patient some space, so the nurses and residents all gathered their things and left Biggie's room.

"Dee, what's wrong? What happened? Is Peaches okay? Sit down. Talk to me. It might help me remember what I needed to tell you. Please just stop crying because, you're making me cry and it hurts to cry." Biggie began to cry into her mouth and the nose tube they gave her for oxygen.

"Wait. I'm sorry I don't want to drop all this on you. Tell me how to do you feel about finding out you're pregnant?" Dee rubbed Biggie's hand in comfort.

"Honestly, I have been trying not to think about it. Dee, I can't even begin to think about myself. I feel like such a hoe. I'm in this hospital bed because I fucked another woman's husband, someone I care for. I accused her of being this nasty ass whore and I go do the same thing to her. Then to add insult to injury, I get pregnant." Biggie placed her hands over her face, shaking her head back and forth.

"So do you want to call Big Rob to tell him what's up?" Dee sat down in the chair beside the bed.

"No. What would I say? I heard you were up here. I'm woke. Oh, yes, although you're married to my co-

worker, I'm having your seventh child. Yippee. Ouch!"
Biggie tried to throw her hands up, but her body was still
in a lot of pain.

Dee chuckled. "Stop it, I don't know how this thing
between you and Rob began, but it has happened and with
everything going on, you need to talk to him. Hell, at least
let him know you're awake. I need to talk to him anyway.
I still don't know if he was the one to hurt G-mama. But I
need to tell him what has happened with Peaches.

"You still think he did it? Wait, what happened with
Peaches?"

Dee knew that Biggie believed it wasn't Rob and
she didn't want to upset her friend in her condition. "I
don't know. It could've been him, Jeremiah, we don't
know."

"I do," Biggie whispered.

"Peaches is in jail. She had a car accident and hurt
some people and ran into a cop car, and she's not herself. I
went to see her after the shop burned down—"

"The shop burnt down? Peaches in jail? What the
fuck is going on? Oh my God! Oh my God, Dee, why are
you just telling me all of this? What day is it? Where the
hell? What? What?"

"Biggie, calm down, please. You're going to upset
your baby. You are not well enough to hear all of this.
Please calm down."

"Fuck that, Dee. Peaches in jail, your shop, you
think Big Rob killed G-mama when I really think it was
this chick that came to the shop looking for her."

"WHAT!" Dee screamed so loud the nurses jumped
behind the desk.

Biggie jumped. "Oh shit! That's what I had to tell you. Oh my god, Dee, I know who killed G-mama. Wait, I remember now. We were looking for G-mama and I decided to go to the shop to see if you would come back there. And this chick came in looking for G. She was kind of creepy. Then we went to view G's body. She was there and she was at the funeral. Dee, I promise she gave me this weird-ass vibe. I never seen her before and I remember she said something to me." Biggie closed her eyes, trying to remember. "Um, um damn. I can't remember. Fuck!"

"Oh shit! If this is true, what do we do? How do we find her?"

"I don't know, but first thing we need to do is get me outta this hospital bed and to my house. I need to collect some things if we're going on a man hunt."

Dee took a deep breath. "Biggie, you need to get well. What are we gon' do both pregnant looking for an unfamiliar face with no leads to where we're hunting? Come on, let's be logical."

"Fuck being logical, Dee, we're all we have right now. And after your last encounter with G, do you really want to let her death be in vein, having her killer live out here with us every day, walking around unpunished?"

Dee took what Biggie said to heart. "It wasn't my fault. I never meant for G to get hurt. I loved her and wanted to protect her. I wanted to protect you all."

Biggie knew she crossed the line. "Dee, look I'm sorry. I didn't mean to imply..."

"Yes you did." Dee rubbed her hands together.

"No, no I didn't." Tears ran down Biggie's cheek.

Dee stared into the distance. "Yes, you blame me. Hell, I blame me kind of too. And Peaches blames me. I know I didn't pull the trigger, but I shoved her out there among the wolves. Why did I do that to her? You're right. We have to find out who killed our girl."

Biggie lay back in her hospital bed. She began to wheeze. "Yes, Dee. Wait, I need to lie back for a minute. I'm feeling nauseous and a little dizzy."

Dee wasn't paying full attention. She was in deep thought thinking about their next move. "And I just might know of a little help we could use."

Biggie pushed the button for the nurse. Before Dee knew it, the door burst opened.

Two nurses ran in. "Oh no, her heartbeat is dropping! She needs fluid. I'm sorry, dear, we need you to step out for a minute. She will be all right. The baby is draining her fluids, that's all. She needs a little rest and she'll be okay. Just wait outside and we'll let you back in after we get her together."

Dee's eyes widened. She walked out the door and watched the nurse close the door in her face. She sat in a chair off to the side and waited as she was told. She decided to go ahead and leave. She knew Biggie was in good hands. Dee needed to get home to get herself together and start working on who this bitch was that killed G-mama.

CHAPTER 7

As Dee walked out the elevator into the underground hospital garage she got an eerie feeling up the back of her neck like she was being watched. She slowly looked from side to side and moved her legs rapidly to get to her car. She looked in her purse for her keys and couldn't find them, but she was too scared to take her eyes off her surroundings. Dee stuck her hands in both pockets, looking for her keys, but they were not there.

She heard footsteps move slowly and heavily behind her. She started to panic. She began to run. As she ran to where she thought she parked, she reached into her pocket again. She saw a shadow on the other side of the garage wall. She pulled her hand out her pocket and her nametag for visiting Biggie fell out. She could feel someone watching her and she didn't know who it was.

"Jeremiah, is that you? Baby, please, you're scaring me." Dee called out in fear, hoping it was him, and then again not.

She reached in her purse again. How could she misplace her keys and where the fuck was her truck? She found her keys in the side pocket of her purse. She quickly hit the key pad to sound her alarm and her truck was parked on the other side of the wall.

Dee ran, jumped into her truck and sped off.

As she hit the curve doing 20 mph in a 5 mph garage, Missy smiled, picked up her name tag and sniffed it.

"Thanks, my pretty. Hmmm, I wonder if this will lead me to Peaches. She in the right place. The hospital is a wonderful place to die." Missy laughed to herself. She got in the elevator, looked at the name tag and pushed the floor that was on the ticket. She smiled at her reflection in the gold doors.

Once the elevator reached the floor, Missy stepped out and started down the hall. When she approached the double doors, she picked up the phone and gave them the name on the name tag.

A nurse asked, "What's the password, please?"

"I'm sorry, my sister just told me she was in here. She didn't give me a password, and she's so emotional she's not answering her phone. Can you please let me pass? I just came in off a plane when I heard about what happened. I'm tired and worried. Please, please, please, she needs family," Missy begged with a weak, sad voice.

The nurse felt sorry for her. "I'm going to let you in this time, but have your sister give you the password. She's is resting now, so you can't stay long. You'll have to come back tomorrow. And we never had this conversation."

Missy smiled an evil smirk and pulled the door as the nurse buzzed her in.

She walked through the double doors and gave the nurse a sad smile. The nurse held her pointer finger up to her lips indicating silence then pointed to Biggie's room. When Missy reached the room, she walked in slowly. She slid her hand across the counter, then on to the foot of the bed and up the side rails. When she looked down into the bed and realized it wasn't Peaches at all, she was pissed.

"You?" Missy questioned to herself.

Biggie was still drugged up and talking in her sleep. "Dee we gotta help Peach..."

"Help Peaches, how?" Missy pretended to be Dee, rubbing Biggie's forehead softly.

Biggie drifted back off to sleep.

This pissed Missy off. She shook Biggie. "What! What does that Peaches need help with?"

Biggie's eyes opened, then closed again.

Missy slapped herself in the forehead. "Where is she? Where is that stinking ass whore? I have to find her so she can get exactly what's coming to her."

The nurse came in hearing Missy screaming. She thought it would be a good idea to check on her. "Hi, is everything all right?" The nurse poked her lip out in sympathy.

"Yes, I just hate seeing my cousin like this." Missy put her hands up to her eyes as if she was crying.

The nurse looked confused. "Your cousin? I thought you said you were sisters?"

Missy realizing, she fucked up so she deepened her cry. "Huh? We are. Why? What did I say?"

"You said cousin." The nurse stood in the door.

"I'm sorry, it's so much going on. I just got off the phone with my cousin, slip of the tongue. You understand when your mind is in a whirlwind?" Missy was hoping the nurse was buying her story or she was going to have to deal with her ass too.

The naïve nurse felt sorry for Missy. "Yes, yes, we get that a lot around here. Can I get you anything? Some juice or soda? Maybe something to eat?"

"Yes, I would love something to drink and eat. After the long flight here and all this, I have worked up an appetite." Missy sat back in the chair and made herself cozy.

When the nurse returned, she had a sandwich, two bags of chips, a cup of fruit, two different kinds of juices and a can of ginger ale.

"I just brought a few things because I figured if you were going to be here for a while you can have something to snack on." The nurse sat everything down on the table beside Biggie's bed.

Missy got up, moved the table closer to her chair, grabbed the remote and started in on her snacks. "Thank you. Yes, I don't know how long I'm going to be here. She keeps talking in her sleep. Has she been saying anything to you, or have you heard conversations she's been having with other family members?"

The nurse looked at the door to see if anyone was coming, leaned against the counter and began to whisper.

"Earlier a lady was here with her boyfriend and it started to get physical. Our head nurse had to step in and ask the guy to leave. I was in here taking her vitals and they were talking about helping one of their friends who was in trouble. But that's all I remember."

"Did they happen to mention the friend's name?" Missy leaned in to see if the nurse would say Peaches.

"No, I can't remember if they said her name, but I do know she is pregnant and it's by someone she shouldn't be pregnant by."

"Yes, Dee is pregnant, but she's pregnant by her boyfriend." Missy rolled her eyes at the nurse, because she really wasn't giving her any help.

The nurse stood up straight, pointed to Biggie. "I'm talking about her."

Missy smiled devilishly. "Oh really? I wonder who this regret of a baby daddy is?"

The nurse looked around and the head nurse was peeking in the door. She knew she had spent too much time in the room with Missy.

"Well, I have to go check on my other patients. If you need anything, just push that button on the remote." The nurse walked out the door.

"Wait. Maybe we can go for drinks later. I could really use a friend and a drink. What time do you get off?" Missy figured she would use the nurse as an inside mark.

The nurse, a young party animal herself, could always use a drink after work. "Sure, me and some of the other nurses go down the street to this bar after work. You can join us, that way you won't be too far and can come back up here with your sister. My shift ends in an hour. I'll come back through when I finish my rounds."

"Great, I don't' know anyone here and I don't really feel like being with family. Some new faces will do me good." Missy smiled and gave a thumbs-up. She sat back in the chair and started on her food. She looked back at Biggie. "I'm going to find out where Peaches is and what your little crew is hiding. G-mama didn't want me and none of y'all going to be together." She laughed to herself.

She sat there and watched television for a while, hoping Biggie would start to talk in her sleep again. She pushed the table back and walked over to the bed.

"Come on, say something. Tell me where is Peaches? I know you can hear me, you little bitch. Tell me where is Peaches, tell me." Missy was hung over Biggie with aggression in her voice. She didn't notice someone had walked in the room.

"Hey! Who are you and what the fuck are you doing to her?" Big Rob's voice was strong and startling.

Missy recognized him and whispered his name. "Big Rob."

"Do I know you?" He looked confused.

"No, yes, I mean, you're Peaches husband, right? I'm a friend of the girls and I remember meeting you before." Missy started grabbing her shit so she could get out of there because he wasn't believing that shit for a minute.

"Naw, I don't remember meeting you. And you didn't look like you were being too friendly with her." He nodded toward Biggie and stepped closer.

"Oh, yes I remember you. I'm really a friend of G-mama's." Missy threw a hard ball, knowing it would piss him off and knock him off his game.

"G-mama? Oh yeah. You must be one of them gay-ass bitches too then, huh?"

"Excuse me?" Missy was pissed.

"Bitch, you heard me. Get the fuck outta here. I don't know what you were doing, but I don't like your kind! And, bitch, you ain't no friend of mine and you don't seem like a friend of hers, so get the fuck outta her before I put your dike ass out." Rob heard G-mama's name and lost his mind.

The nurse ran in the room to see what all the commotion was about.

Missy threw her hands up to the nurse and got outta the room quick. "I'm leaving. Just a family quarrel. I'll be waiting down stairs for you."

When Missy reached the elevator, she leaned up against the doors and laughed for minutes. "Oh my god he was about to kill my ass. That motherfucker wasn't buying my shit at all. He almost caught me. I wanted to start slapping that that big dumb ass Mandingo. I got to find out what Peaches is up to and this pretty little nurse gon' help me. Let me get outta here before more visitors come. What the fuck he doing here visiting her, anyway? Shouldn't he be with his wife? Wait, wait a fucking minute. What is Peaches' husband doing up here without Peaches? Wait, could it be?" Missy laughed hard in her throat. She stepped inside the elevator and calmly leaned against the wall with a big smile on her face.

CHAPTER 8

Jeremiah was pissed. "She running all around town with this fireman, then she goes to a police station and allows herself to be questioned without me. Come on. I'm a lawyer, her fiancé no less. What is she thinking?"

He waited for Dee to pull up and when she did, he was going to get in her ass about it all.

Dee pulled in her driveway and when she saw Jeremiah she knew what time it was. She turned on her womanly charm. "Baby, I know you're upset, but let me explain."

Jeremiah grabbed her arm.

Dee turned and kissed him as hard as she could. "Baby I just need you. Please just put your arms around me and hold me tight. Damn, baby, your body feel so good." Dee smiled at the fact she could use sex as a weapon or a savior in this matter.

"Baby, I don't like... Oh shit that feel good." Jeremiah tried to continue with his rage, but Dee wasn't allowing him to finish.

Dee pulled him in the house while still kissing him. Jeremiah rubbed his hands up her thighs to her ass and cuffed both cheeks, lifting Dee off her feet. He kissed her deep, letting go of all the anger. He let her down and leaned her against the table in her foyer. He started removing her clothes. He rubbed her belly while looking her in the eyes. "You belong to me. This is our baby and you're going to be my wife."

Just as he said that, Dee's mind went into a thought of Christophe. She imagined his strong, powerful body standing at 6'4" with big hands and a beautiful smile. She shivered at the thought of him. This made Jeremiah believe he knew how to touch her, but Dee was not on that same page. Dee tried to fight her thoughts, but she couldn't. There was something about him, her spirit desired Christophe so much.

As Jeremiah fingered her wet throbbing pussy, she imagined it was Christophe. She laid back on the top of the table, raised her knees into her chest and allowed his thick well-manicured fingers to pleasure in and out of her pouring wetness as she screamed and moaned, pushing her pelvis up for him to go deeper inside. She bit down on her bottom lip and squeezed her pussy walls tight as she grabbed both sides of the table trying to fight out the orgasms she was having.

Jeremiah raised from his knees and looked in Dee's face. He noticed a look on her face he had never seen before.

"What were you thinking about?" Jeremiah helped Dee from the table.

Dee felt ashamed so she lied. "What, baby? You. I was thinking about how long it's been since I've had you close to me."

As a lawyer, Jeremiah was paid to know when someone was lying. "Umm."

He grabbed Dee around her waist, kissed her and pushed her against the wall.

"What do you miss most?" He pushed his pelvis into hers and slid upward.

"Um, I miss your kisses, and the way you hold me in your arms, and how you devour my pussy like she's your last meal," she said without eye contact, mostly because the pressure of his body was hurting her.

He kissed her again, this time giving her all of his tongue. He sucked both of her lips and kissed on her neck as he took off her clothes piece by piece. She stood there completely naked as he stared at her.

Dee was uncomfortable. She knew he did not believe her.

"Dee, do you really miss me, or were you thinking about something else, or someone else?"

Dee didn't know where this was going, but she didn't want him to hurt her or her baby. She stepped out to kiss him and he stopped her.

"Baby, tell me the truth. Did you let him touch you?"

Dee sighed in guilt as if it happened. "No!"

"Did he kiss you?"

"No"

"Did you let him fuck on my baby's head?"

"No, baby, he just was being nice. He never touched me, I swear."

Jeremiah pushed her back against the wall. He took his pants off and picked Dee up and pushed his dick deep inside her. He pumped hard and wrapped his arms tightly around her. "Dee, I love you, baby. Please don't ever let another man have you. It'll kill me. It'll drive me out of my mind. You know how I get. You know what I can do, right? Do you understand what I'm saying to you?" Jeremiah cried in her chest as he fucked her soft and held her tight.

Dee didn't know what to do. She stared out into space for a minute, fear filling up her lungs. She wrapped her arms around his neck and said, "I love you, baby. There's no other man for me. You're all the man I want and need."

They made love all the way down the wall to the floor. Dee knew she had to put it on him to take his mind off of her and Christophe. She also knew she had to get back to Biggie and focus on getting Peaches out of jail, so they could find out who killed their friend. She did not need Jeremiah distracting her at all.

She pulled out all her best moves, riding him from the front and back. She sucked his dick deep into her throat, blobbing and slurping all the way down his shaft to his balls, making sure to kiss and lick them softly. Jeremiah moaned in pleasure, remembering the amazing sex he and Dee used to share before all the drama and her bitch-ass friend got in the way.

"Damn, baby, I missed this! Yes, give it to daddy." He curled his toes while grabbing her head from the back, smashing into his crotch.

Dee sucked hard, rotating her tongue around the top of his dick while stroking it at the same time. She moaned and hummed with pleasure in between popping her lips to the taste of him. She sucked, popped, licked, and stroked, sucked, popped, licked, stroked, sucked popped, and licked until he exploded in her mouth. She kissed his body from head to toe. As he trembled to her soft kisses, she led him into the bedroom, laid him down on her plush California king bed and fucked him until he fell into an amazing pleasured sleep.

Once she knew he was in a deep coma-like sleep, she eased out of the bed, trying not to make any sudden movements to wake him. She grabbed her phone, tiptoed across the floor and slipped into the bathroom. She sat on the side of the tub and called Det. Max.

"Hello Det. Max this is Dee. I'm calling because I may need your help."

"Hello? Who is this?" Max was having a sandwich and could not hear Dee between chews.

Dee took a deep breath because she was working on limited time. She elevated her whisper. "This is Dee. You have my friend Peaches there. I know your brother from the fire at my salon. I need your help."

Max dropped his sandwich. "Is this about your friend? Did you find out something I can use to help her?"

"No, well… yes, but not about Peaches' case. It's about my friend G-mama. I mean, Savanna. See Biggie woke up and she believes she knows who killed G, I mean, Savanna and we need your help to find her." Dee heard herself getting loud and began to whisper.

"Wait a minute, wait a minute. I'm not on that case and even if I was, there are procedures that have to be followed," Max explained.

"What? No. Look, you have to help me. Things don't work by procedures and you said if I needed anything to call you. Plus, I need you t…"

Just as Dee was going into what she needed to get Max to help her Jeremiah pushed the door open and stood in the doorframe of the bathroom. Dee was looking down at the floor. She slowing looked up to meet Jeremiah's eyes, which were staring directly into hers.

"Who are you talking to? Him?" Jeremiah stood with his chest stuck out and dick hanging.

"Um, I have to call you back." Dee said into the phone before she slid it down her face in shock to see Jeremiah.

"You really got it for this fireman, huh?" Jeremiah was working up a rage.

Dee forgot to press the end button and Detective Maxwell was still on the line listening.

"I know what you're thinking, but that wasn't him. I didn't want to wake you. See, that was the detective I was speaking with. We're trying to find out what happened to G-mama and I thought he could help…"

Before she could finish her sentence, Jeremiah slapped the taste out of her mouth. Dee fell off the side of the tub and grazed her forehead against the sink.

Detective Maxwell felt the slap. He dropped his receiver to his phone and picked it back up fast. "Dee, are you okay? Can you hear me? Pick up the phone."

But Dee couldn't hear him.

Detective Maxwell grabbed his badge and his gun scrambled over his desk to find Peaches' paperwork which had Dee's address as a point of contact. He memorized the address and rushed out the door.

"Damn it, Dee. Baby, look what you made me do. Why do you want me to hurt you?" Jeremiah walked out the bathroom with his hands up in the air.

Dee grabbed her belly and pulled herself up fast. She wanted to see her next blow coming. She looked around the bathroom to see what she could grab before he came back in there, afraid he was going to hit her again.

"You promised. You promised to never hurt me again. You said you wouldn't hurt me or our baby." She was a little dazed.

Jeremiah looked back at Dee, his stomach soaked into his back with guilt. He felt bad and mad all at the same time, but not at Dee, at himself. He wondered quickly in his mind why his anger took control of him enough to hurt this beautiful woman who was carrying his child.

She leaned over the side of the sink, preparing herself for when he came at her again. She grabbed her stainless steel garbage pail and as soon as he walked back in the bathroom, she swung around, drew her arm back with all her might and popped him across the face with one blow. Jeremiah fell backward and he hit the floor while blood poured out from his head.

Dee stepped back bouncing on her toes from foot to foot like a boxer ready with another blast for him in case he jumped up to rush her.

"Motherfucker, I told you to never put your hands on me again and that's what I meant. I will not let you hurt me or my baby. We 'bout to tear this motherfuckin' bathroom up. Now get up. You want to fight then come on. Otherwise, let me clean you up." She wasn't for his shit. She felt like a beast.

But Jeremiah was not getting up.

Dee thought he was faking. She moved forward slowly and kicked his foot lightly. "Jeremiah, get up. Jeremiah, get up. Get up now!"

Jeremiah was out cold.

Dee started to panic. She walked around him, still afraid he was faking. She couldn't believe it. *I really knocked him out,* she thought to herself. She felt bad. She put her face up to his nose to see if he was still breathing. She could not take another person dying in her life.

He was breathing.

She crawled to the tub, turned on the water, and cupped her hands in it. She crawled back to Jeremiah and sprinkled water in his face.

Dee forced herself to stand up, and worked to get her thoughts together. She went back into the bathroom to get peroxide and gauze, but she caught a glimpse of herself in the mirror. She saw a hand print on her face and a small, bloody scratch on her forehead.

"Motherfucker, look what you did to me!" Dee screamed. "I should've listen to my girls and left you alone, but I didn't want to be alone. But, I've always been alone. All I had was my beauty salon and my girls and now I have nothing."

She sat on the side of the tub and cried, feeling sorry for herself for a few minutes. Then suddenly she stopped. She got up, thought about her girls and realized they needed her. She was not going to let Jeremiah stop her.

She looked at him with disgust. "Fuck you! You can just take a nap right where you are, bitch! I got shit to do and I refuse to let you get in my way."

Dee cleaned herself up, walked out the bathroom, stepped over Jeremiah's limp body, and left him in the middle of the floor.

When Max reached her house, she was gone and so was Jeremiah. He put his hand on his forehead. "What have I gotten myself into?"

CHAPTER 9

Christophe could not stop thinking about Dee. He wanted to do something to help her. He wondered how someone so beautiful could be going through some much. He wanted to take some of the pressure off. But what could he do?

"That's it!" Christophe snapped his fingers once he figured out what he wanted to do. He went to his chief and asked if they could do some community service work.

"Sure it is our district's month to put in our annual services," his chief said. "What do you have in mind?"

Chief knew what Christophe was up to. He invited Christophe in the office to have a long talk with him.

"Well, sir, there's this salon that burned down next door to the coffee shop, and I've met the owner…

Chief cut him off. "Look, Maxwell you're a good kid with a heart of a super hero. I know what you are trying to do. It is big talk around here. I just want you to really take into consideration what you are asking your district to do. See, there's a lot to be done in this community. We can't do personal favors to help you get laid. It might not get the attention you're desiring. I ask you why do you want to do this? If you're asking this of me, I'll do all I can to help to make sure the city backs it up and all the detail of it. But understand this is to help someone. You might not get anything out of this and I need you to be okay with that."

Christophe thought to himself, *why am I doing this*? He sat back in the seat on the opposite side of the chiefs' desk, put his hand up to his chin and took a deep breath. His eyebrows furrowed as he thought long and hard.

The chief cleared his throat.

"Sir, I want to do this because this is our community and a young woman is in distress. Although I find her very stimulating, I would do the same if it were a man. For a person to lose something they put their hard work and money into without notice. Why, it's our job to keep our community supported." Christophe tried to make a strong plea.

"Umm hmm." Chief was not buying any of it.

Christophe knew it too, but stood by his defense anyway.

"Maxwell, I'll tell you what, if you write up the paperwork and get all the details together, I'll submit it to the mayor's office and get you all the help you need. I'll let you lead the project, how's that? Oh and Maxwell, don't make me regret this."

"Thank you, sir. I got this. You won't regret this. You'll have the paperwork on your desk by the end of the day." Christophe's smile spread across his face as he backed his way out of the chief's office.

Before he got out of the chief's office good, a few of his fellow co-workers were all ready to play a trick on him. One of the guys had a pillowcase on his head with Kool-Aid on his lips.

"Oh Christophe, you doing this for lil ole me? My hero." And planted a big kiss on Christophe as if he was Dee.

"Don't you have anything better to do?" Christophe rubbed the kiss off.

But they continued to have their fake wedding. The pillow cased non-bride grabbed his arm and walked him to the end of hallway, where another fireman stood as the minister. The rest of the guys stood as the congregation.

"Dearly beloved, we are gathered here today…" the fake minister began.

The congregation laughed.

But the joke was soon over when the firehouse bell started to ring, indicating a fire was in play. The guys instantly went into hero mode and all the horse play ended. The guys ran and slid down the pole one by one. The men scrambled around hurriedly. Their boots were pulled on, helmets were snatched off the shelves and as they strapped on all their gear. In a few short minutes they were jumping onto a now moving fire truck. As they blazed down the mean streets of Cleveland, traffic was almost impossible to get around. Once they checked the address they realized this fire was out of their district, closer to east Cleveland, but when they pulled up to the fire they see why they had been dispatched. Three other districts were there. The apartment building that was on fire was one of the largest buildings in E.C. and it was quickly becoming engulfed in flames. There were people and children still in the building.

Christophe jumped off the truck. He walked up to the other firemen on the scene. "What's the plan, fellows?"

One of the other firemen turned and looked him up and down. "Oh boy, we have a super hero on deck. Where's your cape?"

Christophe ignored him, turned to the next man and chief. "Sir, do you have a plan? My team will stand by and wait for you to move."

As he said that, a little girl was hanging out the seventh floor window screaming for help.

The other firemen were trying to coach her to jump into the tent. Others were attempting to get in the building, but the fire had taken over the entrance and the whole first floor.

But Christophe, as usual, acts first and thinks about it later. Like an action hero, he jumped up on the bottom balcony, climbed up on the concrete platform, and leaped to the fourth floor balcony where the sliding door was open. The fire did not seem to blazing from the door.

"Who the hell is that idiot and what does he think he's doing?" The chief in charge screamed into his radio.

"That's Maxwell, our team leader. This is what he does. Believe me, he's got this. If anyone is going to save that little girl, he will." Christophe's best friend spoke up for him.

"I don't care what kind of leader he is. No one takes off without my consent." The chief pointed his finger in Christophe's best friend's face.

Meanwhile Christophe reached the little girl's apartment where her mom and little brother were unconscious.

"Ma'am, ma'am, can you hear me? I'm here to save you." Christophe picked up the mother.

He went for the little boy, but when the sister saw him, her eyes filled with tears. She picked up her baby brother and said, "I got him please, don't let us die."

Christophe took a deep breath and said. "Follow me. If you do exactly what I tell you, I'll get you and your family to safety."

He ran out the apartment with the little girl in tow. He went down the same stairs he came up, but the smoke had taken over. With the mother thrown over his shoulder, he pulled the little girl and brother close to his right thigh to cover them from the smoke. The building was falling in from the top and the stairs were shaking from the compact.

Once they reached the fourth floor, he went for the apartment he came out of, but the fire in the next apartment was burning into the hallway, blocking them from getting into that apartment and a fire was flaming up behind them. They were trapped.

The little girl began to cry, while her limp baby brother dangled around in her arms.

"Calm down, I promise I will get us out of here, okay? Just give me a second. Give me a second." Christophe kneeled down so the smoke would not take his breath.

They were stuck in between two apartments. One had water coming from under the door and one had fire coming through the door. He placed the mother down next to the little girl. "Hold her head. Stay right here. I'll be right back." He placed the mother's head on the little girl's leg.

He kicked the door open into the apartment where the water was coming from. The fire was taking over the apartment, but because of the water overflowing from all the faucets, it couldn't take over fully. But this apartment had no balcony, so Christophe grabbed a blanket off the couch, soaked it in water, ran back out the apartment and wrapped it around the little girl and her family. He scooped them all up in one pull, ran them through the fire into the next apartment. Breathing heavily, he sat them down against the sliding door.

"What's your name?" he asked the little girl.

"Christ, and my brother's name is Shug." The little girl still held on to her baby brother."

"Like Christ Jesus?"

"Yes!" She said proudly.

"Well I Christophe our name is almost spelled the same. Okay, Christ, you're going to have to jump onto the tent. I need you to hold on to your brother just like this, so he doesn't break any bones, and jump."

"No, I'm scared. Please jump with me."

"I'll be right behind you with your mom. Come on, we don't have a lot of time. If you don't jump, we will die in this fire. You have to trust me. I promised I wouldn't let you die, didn't I?"

Just as he said that, a big bomb shattered down the front door. Christophe looked around and back at the little girl. He grabbed her up with her baby brother in her arms, ran to the balcony, and threw them both off into the tent.

Christ screamed all the way down, holding on tightly to her baby brother. She landed safely as the firemen pulled her out and grabbed the little brother to give him oxygen and tried to save his life. They waited for Christophe and the mother.

But instead of Christophe coming through the window, a blast of fire shot through the window with a booming rage.

Christophe's best friend ran toward the building, but others grabbed him. "Christophe!" he cried out.

"Mommy!" Christ cried out.

CHAPTER 10

Missy paced back and forth waiting for the nurse to come down so they could meet for drinks and she could find out the truth about why Big Rob was visiting Biggie. She needed more than that. She needed to be in this hospital for days on end to get funky ass Peaches out of the way. But how? How could she become a fly on the wall without being noticed?

Once the nurse reached the lobby, Missy put on her sad family member face.

"I hope you're ready to drown that frown into a drink and turn all the way up?" the nurse wrapped her arm around Missy as if they were old friends.

"I'm ready, Freddy." Missy gave a thumbs-up and rolled her eyes at this chipper ass nurse.

Once they reached the bar, Missy was amazed at all the nurses and residents that seemed to be regulars at this bar. They were turned up, standing on the bar and dancing all over the floor. Apparently, after they leave the hospital they really do need to let loose. Three nurses at the bar were all taking "boiler makers" on while the crowd cheered them through the fire. These boiler makers were made with beer, a shot of Bacardi 151, and fire.

One of the guys Missy knew from the gay bar danced all the ladies off the floor. He was about 5'8" skinny and bowlegged. He was definitely a flyboy, with a short cut dyed pink and blue on the top. He wore tight scrubs and colorful crocs and danced like a stripper. The ladies cheered him on while the male nurses rolled their eyes. But he was well known, so no one bothered him much. When he looked up and saw Missy she placed her finger to her mouth for him to keep his mouth shut. He turned his fingers to his lips as if he was locking and throwing away a key. He figured she was up to know good as always.

Missy made her way to the restroom and he followed in behind her. He said he wasn't going to say anything to anyone else, but he definitely was not gonna let her come in on his scene and not find out what she was up to.

He slipped right into the ladies' room, peeking around the door, making sure no other women were in there to talk shit to him.

He sang her name. "Miiissyy, I know you're in here. What is yo' sneaky lil ass up to now?"

"Look, bitch, you mind your business and I let you keep it, Mikey. Otherwise, I'll do your ass a favor and cut it off for you."

"Uh uh, don't threaten me, Miss Thang. You know I carries me a blade too, Boo Boo. Now dish, bitch." He jumped up on the counter and crossed his legs.

Missy knew he wasn't going to let her go unless she gave him something to feed that gay-ass appetite. "Damn, bitch, okay. You see the nurse I came in with? Well I want to fuck, but she don't know she's gay and I want to get her drunk and open her up to her sexuality."

"Ooooh my goodness. I knew it. You're like my Uncle Ray. Get 'em drunk and take the ass. At least that's how he gets the men." He waved his ass to the side, indicating that his uncle took ass from him.

Missy didn't think that was funny she made a face like she was sick to her stomach and wanted to kill his uncle for him. "Well, when you're ready to take his ass out, call me."

"Aren't we one to judge." He snapped his fingers and smiled.

"I'm not forcing her. She likes me. She's just nervous about what others might think, so I want to make her comfortable." Missy snapped back.

"Well, okay, Miss Thang. Your secret's safe with me. Go get her, mama." He jumped down from the sink.

Just as he was walking out a few nurses were walking in. "Oh my God, this is the ladies' room. What the fuck?"

"Yea, yea bitches. Whatever. Shut up and go empty them drunk lil fishies." Mikey switched his ass and waved his hand as he walked out the door.

When they reached the dance floor, the nurse ran up to Missy. "There you are. I was wondering where you went."

Mikey looked over at Missy, smiled, threw his arm up in the air and switched back to the dance floor.

The nurse looked him up and down and rolled her eyes. "Do you know him? I can't stand gay people. He thinks he's more woman than us." She shook her head.

That pissed Missy off. "No, I don't know him, but you shouldn't judge people. Some people can't help the way they are."

"He can't help it? The Bible says Adam and Eve, not Adam and Steve. It's a lot of beautiful women out here and he wants to be with a man? Yuck," the nurse went on.

Missy wanted to cut her throat. "Well, you know what? That's his business. Let's get some drinks before I lose my mind."

The nurse felt bad going on about so much when Missy was grieving over her family. "You know what? You're right. Let's get fucked up! Wwwwwhhhooooooo. Barmaid, two boiler makers over here, please."

The barmaid smiled. "Oh, looks like I have a new victim, huh?"

Missy smiled. "Or your new best friend."

The crowd of nurses was wowed by Missy's confidence and how easily she fit in. Once the barmaid brought over the drinks, she lit them on fire and the chant began.

"Chug a lug, chug a lug, chug a lug." The female and male nurses chanted the nurse and Missy on.

Missy acted like the drink was too much for her so that she could get the nurse as drunk as possible.

"Oh, you're tapping out?" One nurse in a Hello Kitty scrub jacket laughed.

"Yes, that's a strong drink and hot." Missy smiled a fake innocent smile.

"Bartender, we need a cup of milk her for the baby section." The nurse continued to tease.

Missy was trying to hold her composure. She was not really looking to deal with the entire club, but she made due with the situation.

"Yes, put it in her breast and I'll suck it out." Missy came back with a burn.

The crowd hushed for a moment. The nurse laughed and the entire bar joined in. After that, the DJ turned up the music and the crowd began to dance. The women at the bar laughed and drank as much as they could before joining the other nurses on the dance floor.

Missy seductively put out her hand to the Hello Kitty nurse. "Do you want to dance?"

"Why? You think I'm going to let you suck the milk out my tits on the dance floor?"

"Hey, anything is possible in my world." Missy licked her lips and pulled the nurse to the dance floor.

Missy began to whine her hips and move across the floor and the nurse had sexy moves to match. They danced so intimately everyone began to watch them. This made Missy's nurse upset. She downed her drink and joined them on the dance floor.

"Hey, you came with me. If anyone should be showing you a good time, it's me."

"Well get in here, nurse, and show me what you got." Missy knew her plan would work. Making one nurse jealous by showing interest in another nurse worked like a charm.

"Why do you keep calling me *nurse*? Do you not know my name?" the nurse questioned with drunken desire in her eyes.

"I don't know. Why didn't you tell me your name? Did you not want me to know it?" Missy questioned back in a sensual voice as she danced closer to her nurse.

The Hello Kitty nurse was now dancing on the stage with the DJ shaking her thing all over the place as if she was a stripper in a former life.

Missy got closer and closer to the nurse. The music slowed down and now they were dancing face to face. The nurse's drunken body swayed to the beat and she let Missy whine slowly against her, touching her softly. The other nurses watched in awe, wondering why she was letting this happen, but Missy was alluring.

"Um, this dance is getting a little sexual. We're girls. We shouldn't dance like that," the nurse whispered.

"Why? The music said so. I dance with my sister and friends all the time. It's like listening to a line dance song. You follow what they say. It doesn't mean anything," Missy said convincingly.

"Yes, I guess you're right." The nurse laughed.

"How about we get another drink?" Missy started walking to the bar.

"You didn't finish your first drink."

"That's not for me. I like something soft and sweet." Missy smiled and winked.

The nurse didn't know if it was the boiler makers she'd been tossing back or what, but for some reason she became more and more intrigued with Missy.

"Bartender, do you know how to make any mixed drinks?"

"But, of course, how about my specialty, Sex in the Driveway?"

Missy smiled. "We'll take two."

Five minutes later the ladies took in two more Sex in the Driveway drinks.

"We should go back to my place. I live close, and I haven't drank as much as you. I can drive," Missy said.

"Hey, I thought you were from out of town?" The nurse slurred.

"I am, but my family's place is close by. That's where I'm staying while I'm in town." Missy cleared her throat at her mistake.

"Oh, that's cool. At least you don't' have to pay for those expensive hotels and check out time and wwhhhooo." The nurse started falling off the stool into Missy.
She looked into Missy's eyes and kissed her on the lips. They walked out the club and a few taxi cabs were sitting outside waiting.

"Okay, ladies, y'all know the drill. No one drives home after leaving our bar. Keys in your purses and tell the driver where you're going." The bouncer held the taxi door opened for the ladies.

Once they reached Missy's apartment, the nurse was still turned up. "Put on some music. Let's have another drink." The nurse danced around.

"Are you sure? You seem to have had enough?" Missy sat on the edge of the couch watching the nurse.

"No, I'm off tomorrow and I just want to have a fun."

Missy sat up straight on her seat. "Why don't you take off your clothes?"

"What?" The nurse became uncomfortable.

Missy got off the couch and grabbed the remote to turn on the music.

"Don't you want to get out of those work clothes and get comfortable? I think there's something here. We could both put on our bed clothes."

"Oh yes," the nurse giggled. "I thought you were coming on to me because I kissed you. I don't know why I did that. I think gay people are gross. What possible pleasure can a woman give another woman?"

"Um, so you want some wine?" Missy was getting pissed, but was going to smash anyway, especially because this nurse thought she wasn't gay.

Missy went in the room and acted as if she was looking for bed clothes. The nurse jumped in the shower and Missy put a nightie in the bathroom for her with a towel.

Missy went into the kitchen and poured a glass of wine with a little seduction added.

"Wow! That shower is awesome." The nurse was still drying off when Missy handed her the glass of wine.

"Look, I want to thank you for taking me out to take my mind off of things. I had a really good time."

"Sure." The nurse smiled and sat down on the couch.

The music played slowly. Missy walked in the back for a while, hoping the wine and music would take control of her new flunky. She showered and put on something soft and girly.

When she returned the nurse was standing in front of the speaker slowly grinding to the music. The ecstasy had done its job.

"What are you doing?" Missy acted innocent.

"Dancing. Come dance with me."

Missy loves to seduce women. She did this a lot, but this girl was so dingy and unaware, it was like having a virgin for the first time, she knew she could conquer her and that it would be easy as all the others. Then she thought to herself. *The only woman she could not crush was G-mama.*

"Put your glass down." Missy said seductively.

The nurse quickly drank the last of the wine. Missy grabbed her breasts softly and caressed them gently. The nurse resisted slightly. Missy stepped in closer swaying her hips to the music and the nurse trembled in fear.

"I'm not gay." The nurse blurted out.

"Shhhhh." Missy placed her finger to the nurse's mouth.

Missy pulled the top of the nurse's nightie down really slow.

"Please stop. It's a sin. This isn't right." The nurse spoke, but made no motion to stop her.

Missy licked her nipple that pointed out hard and firm. The nurse gasped for breath. Missy knew then that was her queue. She pushed the nurse against the wall and kissed her very softly. The nurse's pussy was throbbing and she felt embarrassed about it, but never stopped Missy. Missy sucked both her breasts softly and kissed her neck all the way down to her stomach. The nurse moaned in pleasure.

"Has anyone ever licked your pussy before?" Missy asked so softly and sexually.

The nurse's eyes widened. "What? No, please don't do that. I think we should stop this. My father would roll ov..."

Before she could get it out, Missy stuck her tongue out and licked the top of her pubic. Missy opened her legs slightly and used her index finger to rub the tip of the nurse's clitoris.

"Wow, you're really wet. If you really wanted me to stop, you wouldn't be this wet." Missy licked her finger. Missy began to finger the nurse gently and then opened her legs more and placed her warm mouth on her pussy.

"The nurse screamed out loudly. "Oh my God. Why does that feel so good?"

"Because we're women and we know how to pleasure each other. Your body tastes so good. You're really a nice person. If you want me to stop, I will. But you've been so nice to me. I just want to make you feel good. I want you to release all that tension. Can I please?"

The nurse walked away. She went over to the couch laid back and let Missy take her lesbian virginity.

Missy ate her pussy until she came all over the couch. Then she took her in the bedroom. "Have you ever used toys before?" Missy pulled out a box.

"Only a bullet." The nurse was drunk and ready to do whatever Missy said.

Missy pulled out a strap with a big black dildo hanging from it.

"Where are you putting that? That's huge and it's black. I've never seen anything like that. O-M-G!"

Missy strapped up, bent the nurse over the edge of the bed, and played with her pussy with the head of the plastic dick.

The nurse came before Missy could stick it in her. "Wow, that feels so good. I never felt anything like that before. Please don't stop."

Missy inched the dildo inside the tightness of the nurse's pussy. Cum dripped out of her as she screamed out.

"Oh, wait. Please. It's too big. Stop for a minute, please. Please."

"No, take it. You can do it" Missy stroked very slowly, enjoying the pain she was giving the nurse.

The nurse grabbed the sheets really tight, biting down on her lips. "Oh shit. Please."

Missy began to stroke harder and harder all while very gently putting her thumb in the nurse's ass.

The nurse cried out. "Please. Oh my God. Yes…No… Oh please. Oh shit. Oh yes. Please, please, please."

"Ssshhhh. Let me have this tight pussy. You're so wet I want to taste you." Missy stopped stoking and pulled the nurse by her waist to her mouth and began devouring her pussy.

The nurse's eyes rolled in the back of her head. She opened her mouth wide to scream, but she couldn't bring out any words. Missy had sucked the voice out of her.

"Umm, baby, you taste like pineapples." Missy slurped, licked and sucked the nurse's pussy softly like the pro she was.

Tears continued to run from the nurse's eyes. She thought to herself, *I've never been fucked like this before.*

Missy flipped her over, so that they were face to face. With the nurse's juices all over her face, she deeply kissed her in the mouth.

"Climb on top of this dick," Missy demanded.

The nurse rushed to do so. Missy laid down and the nurse climbed on top and inserted the long strapped dildo into her tight pussy. She rocked her hips back and forth, trying to make it fit.

"Oh shit! Fuck, fuck, fuck!" the nurse cried out.

Missy grabbed her ass and slowly bounced her ass to get a riding rhythm. As she pulled her ass cheeks apart, the nurse began to cum in cups.

Missy reached under and put the insert part of the dildo into herself and began to fuck like a beast so that she could get fucked at the same time.

"Oh, yes, move them sexy ass hips. Fuck mommy. Say yes mommy," Missy requested.

"Oh shit, baby."

Missy slapped her hard on the ass. "What I say?"

"Yes mommy! Yes mommy!" the nurse cried.

Once they reached a strong rhythm, they both begin to get massive pleasure. They moaned and screamed until they both hit the climax of a lifetime.

Missy thought to herself, *I could really tame her, but first things first.*

CHAPTER 11

A week had passed and Dee was in a world of her own. Her clients were calling her for appointments, wondering what she was going to do about the shop and wondering what was going on with all the girls.

Dee needed to make things right with her family and with all the running around she was doing back and forth to the hospital for Biggie and trying to get Peaches out of jail, she didn't have time for nothing else, not even her baby.

Her phone began to ring. "Hello"

"Hello, beautiful. I'm sorry to call you out the blue like this, but you've been on my mind."

Dee recognized his voice instantly. She smiled and whispered his name. "Christophe."

Christophe leaned his head against the wall in the firehouse. "So you do remember me? I like that."

"Yes, I remember you. How are you?" She exhaled slowly to the calm of his voice.

"I should be asking you the same thing. The last time I saw you, you were going through so much and I know being in your situation, it has to be overwhelming. But at least you have a man there to help you through it," Christophe hinted.

Dee side eyed her phone, thinking bad thoughts about Jeremiah and catching his hint. "Yes well..."

"Well what? Is everything okay?" He eagerly cut her off.

Dee didn't want to get into it. "How can I help you today?" she said with a smile.

"Well, I understand you're in a relationship, but I was wondering if I could take you somewhere special and show you something, then maybe we could have lunch." He held his breath.

Dee put the phone down to her chest. She thought about all she had going on and needed to do. She closed her eyes and remembered his touch and then put the phone to her ear to say, "No, I'm too busy," but what came out her mouth was. "Yes I would love to be with you. I mean, I would love to go someplace nice with you."

Christophe smiled. "Okay, then it's a date. I'll pick you up at noon, if that's okay?"

"Yes, that's fine!" She jumped up and looked at the time because she was not dressed or bathed.

"Are you okay?" Christophe heard the change in her voice.

"Yes, yes. I'm fine. See you then." She calmed herself.

"I can't wait. What's your address?"

Dee gave Christophe her address. When they hung up, she ran straight for her closet.

"OMG, what to wear, what to wear? I wonder where he wants to take me. Probably to his family's land or something. They seem like they come from money. What if he has a private plane and he takes me to Paris or some shit like that?" Dee laughed out loud. "Pull yourself together. I'm acting like this is a date, and I already have enough going on to be acting like a teenager over some firemen." She slowed herself down and began to search her closet for something casual and comfortable for her and the baby.

She pulled out a cream shirt dress that dipped down in the front and back and some shimmery gray tights. She turned around to grab a pair of shoes and she saw a picture of her and all the girls in the shop. She looked the picture over like it was the first time ever seeing it.

"Look at us. We were all so happy. G-mama's crazy butt, doing the jail man pose. Damn, I miss you, G. I wish you were here. I'm so sorry, G. I'm sorry I let them get you, but I will find your killer, I promise." She sat on the ottoman in her walk-in closet holding the picture close to her heart as tears ran down her face.

She soon got herself together, took a shower, and got herself dressed. After seeing the picture, she really didn't want to go out anymore, but she knew she needed to. When Christophe pulled up, he was nervous. He stepped out the truck wearing a black button shirt that fit it muscle body, some black jeans and a pair Clarks (Shoes). He walked to the door, took a deep breath, then he pushed the doorbell.

"Give me a minute, I'm coming," Dee yelled coming down the stairs.

"Okay, no rush," he yelled back through the door.

Once Dee reached the door, she opened it with a smile she could not control.

"Wow, you even greet in beauty." Christophe complimented.
Dee blushed. "Thank you."
"Okay, are you ready?"
"Ready for what, actually?" Dee questioned

"It wouldn't be a special surprise if I told you." He smiled.

Dee looked at his smile and began to envision her lips kissing his. She looked deep into his eyes and although he was talking for a few minutes, she was in a full daydream of him and his lips kissing all over her pregnant body and making love right in the foyer of her house.

"Dee, Dee, are you okay?" Christophe had been calling her name for a minute.

"Oh, yes, um hmm. I just drifted off for a second, got a lot on my mind." She pointed to her head.

"Oh, well let's hope I can change some of that today." He smiled again.

Dee grabbed her purse and a jacket and then climbed into his truck. As they rode the streets, they talked and talked and shared childhood stories. They laughed and listened to music, reminiscing on old 90's songs. Before long, Christophe stopped the truck.

"I have to put this blindfold you," he said.

Dee looked at him crazy. "Say what now!"

"Dee, I won't hurt you. Please trust me. It's a surprise. Now close your eyes and let me show you that although you've been through something, there are still some really good people out here."

"I want to trust people but since I've been a child I've been hurt by people I should've trusted. I'm sorry, but I can't let you blindfold me." Dee looked at him with puppy dog eyes.

Christophe leaned over in his truck and put a deep passionate kiss on her. "I'm sorry. I couldn't help myself. I hope I didn't step out of line."

Dee took in a deep breath and exhaled again.

"Please trust me. If at any time you feel uncomfortable, I promise I'll take it off." Christophe looked her deep in her eyes.

Dee closed her eyes and turned her body toward the passenger door. Christophe placed the blindfold on her and started to drive toward the destination. Once they pulled up, he said, "Sit right here. I'll be right back."

Dee wanted to take off the blindfold to peek to see what was going on, but decided not to. Before she knew it, her door was opening and she could smell the flavor of rich coffee. The smell was familiar.

"Okay, Dee. I want you to put your arms around me and I'm going to help you out the truck." Christophe had a smile on his face as wide as the sea.

"What, wait. What if I fall?" Dee was reaching her hands out like a blind man.

"I won't ever let that happen. If you want, I could carry you out," he said.

"No, you can't. I'm too thick in my hips for you to do that." She chuckled.

Before she knew it, he scooped her up in his big, strong arms and held her close to his chest. Dee didn't say another word. She wrapped her arms around him like Lois Lane from Superman and let her hero take her to her surprise.

"I just want you to know I had a lot of help with this and I really hope you like it." He leaned his head close to hers.

"After all I've been through, I'm sure whatever it is, it'll be a rainbow in the dark." She could smell his cologne and unlike Jeremiah's, it wasn't making her sick.

As soon as she thought about Jeremiah, her stomach tightened. She had shit to do, and a man and here she was acting like a Disney princess looking to be rescued.

Christophe placed her down very gently on the ground. She could hear people moving about around her. But as long as she was with him, strangely she didn't feel scared.

He started removing her blindfold. "I hope you like it."

"Like what?" Dee turned around.

Christophe pushed the door open to Dee's shop and the whole place had been cleaned up and remodeled from the fire.

"Oh my goodness. Oh my God! What did you do?" She turned to Christophe with tears in her eyes.

"Surprise!" A group of firemen rushed over to them.

"Whew!" Dee jumped, startled from the loud voices.

"Ma'am, Maxwell really wanted to help you out so some of the fire brothers pitched in and we got some contracts from the city to do you a solid." The chief handed Dee a bouquet of roses, and winked.

"Thank you. I can't believe this." She walked through her shop.

"We know it's not the same, but for a handful of fellows, we did our best," Christophe's best friend chimed in.

His wife, who was also there, added, "Yes, don't worry. They called me in for a woman's touch. We got you some hair dryers, blow dryers, marcel curlers, and iron stoves, a few flat irons and chairs and all different types of every hair product you could name. A few dozens of towels. Because I know that's very important, a microwave and coffee maker, a small refrigerator and some more knick knacks and whatnots."

The little white woman, who was married to Christophe best friend, was in control, waving her tight firm arms back and forth and around, showing Dee everything her shop held.

Dee was paying attention, but was so touched and overwhelmed she could not hear too much of anything. She turned toward Christophe and looked into his eyes. She knew there was something special about him from the moment they met. She wanted to hug, kiss, make love to him, but she had too much drama going on in her life to cross him up into it. He smiled a nervous smile as he leaned against the glass pane door.

"Now you have everything you need so you can make all you clients as beautiful as you again," Christophe blushed as he spoke.

Dee's heart dropped. She turned back around and exhaled as she looked at all the workstations. "Not everything."

A feeling of grief and hurt came over Dee as she noticed the little white woman sitting in G-mama's station. She became instantly breathless.

"Excuse me, wha, what's your name again?" Dee held her belly.

"It's Chrissy. Oh my goodness you're with child. Are you okay? You want me to get these boys outta here?" she asked in a country singer accent.

"No, but that's G-mama's space. Can you please get up?" Dee snapped a little.

Chrissy's feelings were slightly hurt. "Well, excuse me. I was going to suggest doing some work for you, if you were looking for stylist, but I can see you're a bit rude."

Christophe jumped in. "Chrissy, Chrissy wait. G-mama was the young lady that was murdered I told y'all about. They were like sisters."

Chrissy's face turned red. "Oh my goodness. Please forgive me. My dear, you have been through so much. Christophe told me and my husband all about you and we are so sor…"

Her husband Christophe best friend bumped his wife and slid his arm around her waist. "Baby, give it a rest."

"Okay, chocolate drop. He has to shut me up sometimes." Chrissy smiled.

"I apologize. It's just I haven't had time to process it all yet and with everything going on, it's all a little too much, you know?"

"It's just fine. Well think about if you want some girls in here to work while you handle your business. I grew up in a shop in my mama's garage back in Texas and I will be willing to come and manage your shop, get some girls in here, pay you booth rent, and work a chair for you. You never know, we might be double dating real soon." Chrissy grabbed Christophe's arm.

"Baby." Her husband shook his head, notifying her she was crossing the line again.

As everyone gathered in the back where they had finger foods set up, Christophe walked up to Dee, who was admiring her space in sadness. He placed his hands on her shoulders and in a swift turn, she faced him with her face in his chest. He placed each hand on both sides of her face, leaned down and kissed her thick, shiny lips with the passion of a beast, but the softness of a rose.

As they stood by the large storefront window, Jeremiah rode by on his way to Dee's with roses and a gift for their baby to apologize for what happened between them days before.

CHAPTER 12

The next morning at the hospital Big Rob sat staring at Biggie. When she opened her eyes, she thought she was dreaming.

"Hey you?" she weakly muttered.

"Hey you. I'm sorry this happened to you. It's all my fault." He hung his head low.

"No, no. I knew what I was doing. I have made so many mistakes, but you are not one I regret." Biggie tried to roll to her side, but was in too much pain.

"What about the baby?" He moved in closer.

Biggie lifted her hand to rub her stomach, but then stopped herself. She looked over at Big Rob and he had tears in his eyes. He sat back in the chair on the side of the bed, put both his hands up to his face and inhaled deeply.

Biggie pushed the button on her remote control to lift the head of her bed.

"Rob, things happen. It's called life. I've never connected with anyone the way I connected with you, and although it's extremely wrong, I would not change a thing. Being in here, in and out of consciousness, has given me a lot of time to think. And with all that has happened I need to learn to appreciate all things, good or bad."

"Baby, I'm married with children. I have a cheating, gay wife. I abused her and took advantage of you in my time of anger and distress." Big Rob looked down at the floor.

"Come here, we did this and we will get through this. If it's not together, we will remain friends. At first, yes, you scared the shit out of me, but we gave each other what we needed." Biggie kissed his hands as he sat on the side of her bed.

"So is Peaches still at Dee's?" Big Rob wondered.

"What? You don't know. Peaches is in jail. She had a bad car accident and Dee's trying to find a way to get her out. Oh shit and I know who killed G- ma—" Biggie stopped herself.

Big Rob looked like a ship hit, when she mentioned Peaches name.

"I'm sorry, I know you're mad at her. But she is my friend, your family, and I love her, and I know you do too. Wait. Are you still a suspect?" Biggie pushed herself upright.

Rob changed the subject. "Peaches is in jail? Where? Why? What?"

Biggie knew that he should be upset, but in that moment she couldn't help her human instincts to feel a little jealous.

Rob saw it in her face. "I'm sorry, but she is my wife, the mother of my children."

Biggie rubbed her stomach subconsciously. She thought to herself, *this is why it doesn't pay to have an affair of any kind because in all cases with a real man you'll come out second best.*

"You have to contact Dee. She has all the information. I have some information myself. Wait for me. I'm coming with you." She weakly attempted to pull the covers back.

"Yo, yo, yo, ma. You have to stay in this hospital bed. First off, you're too weak to move and I don't think you can be released yet. Don't the doctors have to do that or something? Plus, you have my baby inside of you. I don't want anything else to happen to you or it." Rob rubbed her forehead.

Biggie smiled at the fact that he cared for her and the baby. Just then, the nurse walked in. She set the chart on the counter as she prepared to check Biggie's vitals. She dropped her gloves and picked them up and started to put them on. Biggie watched her from the bed as she was giving Big Rob details about how to reach Dee about Peaches.

"Excuse me, nurse, please don't put on those gloves you dropped on the floor." Biggie whispered in a soft calm voice. But the nurse didn't turn around. She kept prepping.

"Rob, you have to help Dee get Peaches outta there. She won't survive," Biggie pleaded.

The nurse moved in closer. She rubbed down Biggie's IV. She stood at the machines and wrote in the chart. Biggie gave Rob Dee's phone number and address. "I have to clean your line." The nurse took a needle with clear liquid and pushed it into the IV line to make sure it was clear. Biggie began to slur in her speech. She tried to speak clearly, but something would not let her. But she kept speaking to Big Rob.

"I think I know whooo, G-mama, deea..." She was out like a light.

"You think you know what, baby? You okay? Yo, what happened to her? What did you do? What the fuck?" Rob was upset at the sight of Biggie passing out like that.

"Oh, she's been in and out like that since she's been here. I think she began to get too excited. You might want to leave and come back later." The nurse spoke through her hospital face mask.

"Okay, I got some things to take care of anyway. Yo, do me a favor. Tell her I'll be back when she wakes up.

"Okey dokey." She saluted him.

Rob did not want to leave Biggie. He stared at the nurse. He didn't know her, but he had a weird vibe about her and just couldn't put his finger on it. And with all the shit he was just hit with from Biggie, he had no time to really go through it now. So he kissed Biggie on the forehead and left.

The nurse walked in. "Hey lover, did you surprise your sister? Did she get a kick outta you coming in here as her nurse? Wait, what are you doing with that needle? That can be dangerous. If my head nurse walked in and found you with that I'd be in big trouble."

Missy pulled the mask under her chin. "Be cool. It's just water. I thought it would be funny."

"Oh, well put it away. I have to take her vitals and change her bandages. You have to step outside until I'm done." The nurse turned to the chart.

"I'm staying in here with you." Missy grabbed the nurse's ass seductively and kissed her on the neck.

"Stop that, I'm at work. No one here needs to know what happened between us. I'm not gay. And I don't want people looking at me in that way." The nurse gave attitude to Missy.

"You weren't saying that last night or this morning when I was fucking you and you were laying in my bed screaming my name. What would they think of that? What would they think of you signing into work just to be here with me when you know you are supposed to have the day off? What would they think of you giving me this nurse's outfit and needle, allowing me to have this patient's chart? You're my bitch and I'll touch you how I please. That pussy belongs to me. Fuck them. Do you understand me?" Missy walked all the way up on the nurse and pinned her to the counter.

The nurse moved over. "Why are you so angry? I just want to protect my job."

"I'm not angry. You just hurt my feelings." Missy ran her hand through the nurse's hair.

"I'm sorry. I thought you would understand." The nurse calmed with Missy's touch.

"I'm sorry too. Now give me a kiss." Missy smiled.

Just as the nurse was about to kiss Missy the dietary staff peeked in. "Is she ready for breakfast yet?"

The nurse jumped. "No, she is still asleep, but you can bring in the tray, put it on her table. Maybe she'll wake up wanting to take something light."

The dietitian walked the tray. "So we have a new nurse on the floor? Cool. Hi, I'm Mo. Didn't I see you at the nurse's bar the other night?"

Missy really wasn't trying to make new friends, but lil Miss Mo held her hand for two Mississippis as she shook her hand.

"Yes, you did."
Mo was a little tomboyish with dreads, but she had the prettiest smile and deep dimples. She also had a big ass and tight legs with pretty teeth and light brown eyes. She put Missy in the mind of G- mama. Missy thought about

G-mama and anger filled her belly. She remembered the reason she was here. She had to get that chart from the nurse.

As the dietitian and Missy spoke, the nurse took Biggie's vitals. She noticed some information written down in the chart that didn't make sense. She wrote it on the back side of the last page and continued to do her job.

Missy asked to help as Mo left the room. The nurse wasn't paying attention to the flirting that went on between them. But she was starting to get a bad vibe about Missy. Once the nurse put down the chart, Missy grabbed the page and stuffed it into her pocket. The nurse got a bedpan from the cabinet and filled it with soap and water. She pulled a rag out of the drawer and began to wash Biggie up.

"I can do that. I mean, she my family. Why don't you go check on your other patients and let me finish up here, so that we can spend more time together later." Missy grabbed the rag from the nurse.

"Okay, thanks, lover," she whispered. She picked up the chart and walked out. She noticed the top page was missing, but she did not say a word.

Missy didn't finish the job. She dumped the water into the sink and walked back over to Biggie.

"Now you belong to me, and when you wake up, you're going to tell all about Ms. Peaches and where she is. You're gonna tell me what you know and then I'm going to kill you." Missy leaned in and mimicked Big Rob's kiss on the forehead.

CHAPTER 13

Dee woke up to Christophe looking her in the face. They both fell asleep in the shop on the soft, leather couch in the waiting area.

"Wow, you're so beautiful. Even when you're asleep," he complimented her.

"Oh my, when did we fall asleep? What time is it?" She rubbed her eyes and rolled her swollen ankles that were stretched across his lap with her heels still on her feet.

"It's early. Oh wow, look you ankles. You shouldn't have fell asleep with your shoes on." He removed her shoes and began to give her a foot rub from her ankles to her toes.

She didn't fight it. She leaned back on her arm folded under her head and moaned. "That feels amazing. Thank you."

"I'd do anything for you. I can't understand why your fiancé` doesn't do this for you."

Dee tensed up and moved her feet away. She had forgotten everything. She just had the best sleep she'd had in weeks and shared a moment with a man that was not her psycho fiancé. She loss focus on what she should be doing to find G-mama's killer and getting Peaches out.

"I'm sorry did I cross some kind of line?" He knew he had.

"Yes, we both have. I'm pregnant, I'm engaged and I have a mess going on in my life. I appreciate all that you've done, but this shouldn't be happening. It cannot happen. Whatever you're going for can't happen." She threw her hands up.

She tried to get up, but her swollen ankle stopped her from jumping up in the manner she wanted to. He helped her up and pulled her close.

"Stop it, you're going to hurt yourself. I know you're pregnant. I know you're engaged, but I can't help the way I feel for you. I know that's makes me a idiot, but my father always taught me and my brother to follow our hearts, even though I know it might hurt me. I want to help you. I want to be here for you. I, I lov…"

His phone began to ring his brother's ring tone. "Excuse me." He was glad because he was about to tell her he loved her.

"Bruh, what's going on?" He answered in his urban hipster voice.

While he was on the phone, Dee took the opportunity to check her phone. She looked around for her purse and wobbled her swollen pregnant ankles over to it to get her phone from it. She had put it on vibrate because she cannot stand when someone is on a date or spending time with a person and they are constantly on their phones. Plus, she didn't want it ring and give her worse news, nor did she want to hear from Jeremiah.

Christophe turned to her. "Yes, she's with me now. We're at her shop."

When Dee reached her phone, she saw she had a number of phones calls from Jeremiah and test messages. She was bracing herself emotionally, so she didn't too much pay attention that Christophe mentioned her to his brother or that his brother asked about her, even. She shook her head. *If Jeremiah knew I was here with Christophe he would kill both of us.* She pressed messages to check what he wanted, but before she could get the last text: "I'm going to kill you both," her phone rang.

Max was telling Christophe how he was on the phone with Dee the other day and she dropped her phone so he heard all the ruckus in the background. "Little brother, I think this guy is dangerous. When I reached her house no one was there, but I did find blood in the bedroom. I didn't pursue it because she has enough going on, and when you told me you were seeing her the other day, I figured she was fine, but I need you to stay away from her."

Dee answered her phone.

"Hey Dee, this is Big Rob. I need to know what's going with Peaches."

"What, bruh? Wh…" Christophe questioned his brother.

But before he could finish his question, Jeremiah came rushing into the door with a vengeance.

Dee, startled by the door bursting open, dropped her phone and screamed.

Jeremiah rushed Christophe and knocked his phone out of his hand.

Max dropped the phone at his desk, jumped over his chair and made a mad dash out the precinct and into his car. He was speeding over to Dee's shop. He called for backup once he reached the street.

Jeremiah, now on top of Christophe, was beating him in the face. Punch after punch Christophe began to bleed from his face.

Dee stood there in shock. In her mind, she was screaming "Stop! Get off him. I love him!"In reality, she could not move for what seemed like hours. Finally something clicked and she came to her right mind.

"Stop, Jeremiah. What the fuck are you doing? Get off him."

"Get off him? Get off him?" He straddled Christophe like a wrestler. "You taking up for him?"

Christophe flipped Jeremiah off him and pushed him across the room. They both struggled to their feet.

Christophe kicked his long leg up and caught Jeremiah in the face. He turned to Dee as he wiped the blood from his mouth. "Are you okay?"

Jeremiah rushed him from behind and they fought like two wild lions fighting for pride territory. They pushed Dee into the station. She fell and hit her head and began to bleed. She saw her phone under the chair and grabbed it to call the police.

"Hello, hello, who is this?" She asked in a dazed voice.

"It's Rob. Yo, you okay? What's going on? I know you're pregnant. Do you need help? Where are you?"

"Help!" she muttered as she passed out.

Christophe rushed to her. "Dee!"

"Get your motherfuckin' hands off her." Jeremiah pushed Christophe away.

"Dee, Dee. You all right? Bitch, you better be all right, you better not lose my baby. See what you get when you're up here with this trash? Dee, baby, damn wake up. I promised I wouldn't hurt you. See what made me do. Why do you keep making me do this to you? You stupid bitch, wake your ass up!" Jeremiah shook her like a rag doll.

Christophe hit me with a straight punch and knocked him silly. Jeremiah dropped Dee and shook his head to regain consciousness. He scrambled around over the floor in his own blood trying to reach his feet.

When he reached his knees, Max rushed in, gun out. "Freeze! Get up and put your hands up."

"Hold up. I'm a lawyer. This is my fiancé and this motherfucka was in here taking advantage of her. Put the gun down. He's abusing his position as a fireman, confusing a pregnant woman and attacking a city official. Arrest him, officer!" Jeremiah tried to plead a case.

"You all right, bruh?" Max looked Christophe over, not paying Jeremiah any attention.

"Bruh?" Jeremiah's eyes darted from Max to Christophe. "Oh, I see. What? Y'all from the same fraternity? Got each other's back, huh? Well i…"

"Shut up. You're under arrest, motherfucka, and to answer your question, this is my real brother. You're lucky I don't let him beat your ass and take your woman," Max said with a smirk.

Jeremiah's anger took over. He dropped his hands. "Let's get it. Don't let this suit fool you. I'm from the streets."

Max's backup came in. "Are you all right, Detective?"

"Yeah. Cuff this fool and get him outta here. And let's get a ambulance in here for this woman."

Christophe turned to Dee and swooped her up in his arms. He laid her on the couch.

"Chris, you shouldn't move her."

"I can't leave her down on the floor. Get a towel over there for me and wet it so I can put it on her head. Damn! This shop has seen some things. Bruh, she told me a lot of shit last night about what she's been through and she has a lot of information for you about her girl that's locked up and about the girl who was murdered. You have to help bruh. Please, for me. Please?" Christophe looked at Dee then back at his big brother.

Dee began to come through. She jumped up.

"Take it easy, little lady." Max looked down at her.

"Detective! Christophe. You have to help him. Jeremiah is very strong. He'll kill anybody that gets close to me. He…"

"He is under arrest and Christophe is fine. I taught my little brother well. Believe me, he knows how to handle himself."

Christophe sat down beside her. "Are you okay?"

She was more embarrassed than anything. She looked down at her belly and then at the blood on her hand. "Look, I'm not one of those women that thinks I deserve to be abused. I don't want you to think I'm weak or hard up for someone to love me because I'm not beautiful or because I'm plus size. He wasn't like this when we first fell in love. And he promised to get help. He was all I had while going through this. He…"

"You don't have to explain anything to me. I won't ever let him hurt you again." Christophe grabbed her hand and placed it on his heart.

"Yo, bruh, the EMS is here. Come outside and let me talk to you for a minute, while they get her together." Max gave Christophe that same big brother look he gave him at the precinct.

"I know what you're going to say, but save it. Dad taught us to follow our hearts. You know it. I don't know what happened to you, but I love him and mom's story of how they fell in love meeting on Monday and marrying the following Sunday and I know she's the woman for me. I feel it in my heart. She needs someone and that someone is me." Christophe pointed to his chest.

"Chris, this girl is bad news, bruh. Shit is falling apart around her like flies to shit. I don't want to look up and you're one of those dead bodies, or getting put in jail, or some crazy shit like that. She needs an exorcism or something, bruh." He was serious, but chuckled at his reference to the Exorcist movie.

Christophe gave him a sharp side eye.

"Wait, I thought this shop burned down?" Max realized it was renewed.

"I called in a favor with the city and the firehouse." Christophe said like a little boy.

"WHAT! What is this girl doing to you? Are you serious? Did the fire report even come in on this? What are you doing lil brother ? Damn it. I don't want to have to clean up your mess. Look, leave this girl alone. She's blocking your better judgment." Max was now pissed.

"What happened to you, bruh? Mom always told us to be there for people in need, and to worry about our fellow man. And…"

Max cut him off and grabbed his shoulder. "The only person I need to worry about is you. You're my little brother and I don't want shit to happen to you. What's the matter with you? Leave this girl alone or I promise you…"

"What? You promise me what? You're not the boss of me. I'm a grown man, Max."

"Or I won't help her," Max threatened.

Christophe exhaled. He turned his brother to look into the shop. "Bruh, she's a young pregnant woman with no one. Do you really want to make that threat? Because I will not leave her alone. I *will* help her. Are you really going to let me do this alone?"

CHAPTER 14

A week later the shop was back jumping with Chrissy and the other four workers she brought in with her— Ivory, Mary, Wanda, and Angie.

Chrissy had the shop running like a well-oiled machine. She was happy to do it. Being a stay-at-home wife and mom with a husband for a fireman, she really had not had much to do, but take care of her family, which she loved. But it was nice having somewhere to go and having people count on her. Although Heavenly Hands was not her shop, she was going to run as if it was. She planned to make Dee and her husband so proud of her. Her mother's shop catered to all cultures of women, so she could do hair of any kind. However, she knew she was going to have to prove it. Because when she called all the clients of the girls, and told them the situation and how she and the ladies of her PTA group who all worked in salons before were going to take over, a lot of the clients were skeptical. But Chrissy, with her country persuasive voice, got them into the shop. A lot of the ladies had not had their hair done in weeks and loved the shop and wanted to support Dee in any way they could. They trusted Dee, so they decided to give it a try.

Dee didn't want to give up control of her shop, even temporarily. But she knew she had to, for herself and for her clients. She, Christophe and Max were working together to get to the bottom of G's murder. Max had gotten all the information he needed from Biggie. Since it was only hearsay, he could only work off shift, because the chief would have his ass if she knew he was working on a case that wasn't assigned to him. But he wasn't going to let his little brother go through this alone.

~~~~~~~~~~~~~~~~~

"No, get the fuck outta here. Bring her back. What did you do with her? Where's G? Where's G-mama? What did you do with her? You bitches took her from me!" Peaches screamed at the top of her lungs as she held a broken piece of plastic from her lunch tray.

The officers surrounded her, ready to attack as soon as one of them saw an opportunity.

The older female officer wanted to save her. "Come on, sweet baby, calm down and put that there down before these folks kill you damn it."   Officer Mae Lewis held both hands out, protecting Peaches and her fellow officers.

"I want G-mama. They took her from me. She's been here with me every day and now she's gone. They think I'm crazy, but I'm not crazy, crazy." She twitched as she spoke, watching every corner of the room.

"I know, I know you're not crazy. Would a crazy person know how to lay that hair out so pretty without a comb or hair grease? Honey hush. You just need to calm down, precious."

Peaches rubbed her hands through her hair. "G did my hair. She wanted me to look pretty when it's time for me to go home."

"Oh well, now see, maybe she had to leave to go get home ready for you. No one took baby. She's gone to get prepared for you, sweetness."

"She did? Yes, that's just like G. She loves me. She's always doing stuff like that."

Peaches instantly forgot about the officers that surrounded her and dropped the plastic and drifted off into lala land.

A bold and cocky female officer rushed Peaches to the floor and cuffed her with aggressive procedure. "Stupid bitch, get yo' crazy ass up. Made me miss my lunch."

"You don't have to do all that. She's not in her right mind, honey," Officer Lewis defended.

"Shut the fuck up talking to me. I'm not here to make these damn people my friends. I'm here to do a job."

"Honey, you can't treat people like animals. They're human beings." Officer Lewis pleaded.

"Well this one needs to be put with the animals in the Hanna House. She don't need to be here wasting our time." The aggressive officer roughed Peaches up off to the hole.

"Wait, she has a visitor. That's why I came in here. What am I going to tell him?" Officer Lewis made a sad face.

The aggressive officer said, "Not today she doesn't."

Officer Lewis went to the front desk and made a call.

The female sergeant down in visitation picked up the phone and took the call. She looked over her glasses at Big Rob, cleared her throat, and hung up the phone. "Sir, excuse me, sir. Yes you. Yes, the young lady you came to visit can't have any visitors right now."

"What? I've been sitting here for almost two hours waiting. Why the fuck not?"
She took a deep breath, looked over her glasses again. "I don't know why, sir. I got the call, I told you what I know, and that's that."

"Y'all rude as fuck up in here. I just found out my wife is in jail. I had to wait a week to get approved to see her, and then I get here and y'all keep me waiting for two hours, just to tell me I can't see her." Big Rob threw his hands up and walked off.

As he was leaving out, Dee was coming in. "Big Rob, you made it. How is she?"

"I don't fucking know. They wouldn't let me see her. If that's what you're here to do, you should forget it about it. They on some fuckery."

"No, I mean, yes, but I have to handle some other business as well, which may help find out who murdered G."

Big Rob blew his breath in disgust.

"I know you don't want to hear it, but this can help you too. And let's not forget, you're not innocent in all this either." Dee rolled her eyes.

"Yeah whatever. Y'all fucking girl seduced my wife and… and you know what. It doesn't matter. Let me ask you something before you piss me off."

Dee started to walk away because he had already pissed her off.

He lightly grabbed her arm. She looked at him with disdain.

He threw his hands in truce. "I apologize. A lot is going on, but I have to ask you something about Biggie. When you go to see her, does she always dip in and out on you?"

Dee was confused. "What do you mean?"

"Does she be awake and then asleep again."

Without questioning it, Dee said, "Yes, it's the medicine they gave her, that's why. Wow, you really care for her, don't you?"

"Yeah, I do." Big Rob blushed and looked ashamed at the same time.

"I wish that could flatter me, but it doesn't. What you're doing is wrong."

"Yeah whatever. Y'all should've been telling my wife that while y'all let her sit up there fucking that dike bitch."

"We didn't know. Look, I got shit to do."

"I bet. I just was worried about the fuckin' nurse that was there the other day, but I can't fucking talk to you stupid bitches without getting pissed off."

"Bitch! Fuck off and stay away from Biggie. And try not to beat your kids how you did their mother."

That comment made Rob feel like shit. He hated his self for how he did Peaches and he had not been able to be around the kids since everything happened. But he knew he needed to get them from his parents' house soon. He didn't know how he was going to explain to them why mommy wasn't home. He walked away without saying another word.

Dee walked into the building where Detective Max and Christophe were waiting for her. As they sat going over all the details from Dee and Biggie, Dee began to get emotional.

Christophe rubbed her back. "Are you okay, beautiful?"

Max rolled his eyes and Dee saw him. She leaned in to move Christophe's hands off her back and focus her attention on the little evidence they had. She felt the negative energy from Max and she couldn't blame him. Just going over everything that has happened, she knew she needed to get Christophe interest off her, but she did not know how to do it without hurting his feelings.

"Max, in my office now!" the chief called out her office door.

Max rolled his eyes and exhaled an aggravated breath. He slowly got up from his desk. "I'll be back. Dee, if you think of anything else write it down. Bruh, keep your hands off of her."

He reached the chief's office. "Yes, sir?"

She slammed the door behind him. "What the hell is this I hear you arrested a man a week ago and he's still in lock up? He's causing a ruckus, screaming he's lawyer and you had them keep him from release and refused to give him a phone call?"

Max didn't say a word. He just stood there with a light smirk on his face.

"Explain!" the chief yelled.

"Chief, this dude is bad news. He's a woman beater and possibly a murderer."

"And how do you know this?" She looked through her blinds to his desk.

"I witnessed it, sir."

"Detective, why is your brother here in my precinct again? And isn't that the woman that you were with a few weeks ago? What is going on here?" Chief squinted her eyes like she smelled something fishy.

As Max explained to the chief, Dee felt it was the perfect opportunity to talk to Christophe.

"Christophe, we need to talk. This is not easy for me, but I think we need to talk about the elephant in the room."

"What's wrong, beautiful? You want to get something to drink or eat in the break room?"

"Yes." Dee loved the sound of food.

They walked into the break room and Christophe made a coffee for himself and got a donut and chocolate milk for Dee. He placed everything on the table and turned to Dee.

"What's on your mind, beautiful?"

She rubbed her hands nervously together. "That you have some strong feelings for me, and um well, that's not good."

He walked up close to her, making her walk backwards. "Why?"

"Because you don't know me and because I have too much going on in my life. I'm bad luck. And because your brother hates me. I'm engaged and pregnant, and I know I sound like a broken record, but…"

Christophe smiled and walked closer, forcing Dee into a corner close to the wall. "Dee when I first saw you, I knew."

"Knew what?" She had no more room to move back.

"I knew you were the one. I know you have some things going on, but it's nothing God can't take away. We're going to find your friend's killer. We're going to get this dude outta your life, and we're going to make you believe again."

"You don't understand. Jeremiah will never let go of me, and especially his child. He's a great lawyer. He will make sure he always plays a part in my life."

"I don't want to take you from him and I would never stop a man from being a dad. I know you will come to me, our souls belong to one another." He leaned down and kissed her.

Dee tried to push him away, but couldn't fight it. She felt the passion he had for her and she loved his kiss. She wrapped her arms around his neck and he pulled her up off her feet. They fell into the wall and right there in the police break room they devoured each other's mouth for five minutes.

Max walked in and cleared his throat. "What the hell are y'all doing? This is a police station, not a high school. Bruh, you're really fuckin' up. I can't sit here and wait for you to fuck up your life with this girl. She's bad for you. I know it and if you would get your head out your ass, you would see it too." He stared at Dee's sad eyes. "Look, no offense, but you got too much shit going on in your life. I don't want my brother to become a victim of your cursed lifestyle. I'll continue to help you, but only on the terms that when we're done, you stay the fuck away from my little brother."

Dee started crying. She knew he was right, but it still hurt to hear.

Christophe was furious at Max actions and tried to comfort Dee.

"Christophe, he's right. This is what I have been trying to tell you. I need your brother's help and I appreciate you and I do …"

"What? You appreciate me? Dee, you love me. I feel it and so do you. Nothing's perfect and things are going to happen in life that we can't explain. And my brother doesn't understand or believe in love. I'll wait for you, but I won't walk away from what I know is true." He held her hand and kissed it softly.

This made Dee melt, but she knew she had to stop it. She walked over to Max. "I want your help. I'll do what you ask. Can you please take me to see Peaches?"

Christophe did not turn around to watch them walk away. Max knew his brother was hurt and angry, but he was glad his words got through to Dee, because he didn't know what he would do if something happened to his only brother.

When they reached the building where Peaches was being held, Max walked up to the officer at the desk. A minute later he told Dee, "Come on, we have to go downstairs. Something happened."

Dee's heart dropped. "What happened? We can't see her? What's wrong? Where is she?"

Max put his hands in his pockets. "Calm down. Yes, we can see her. I'm a detective. I can get into any place in this building. I don't know what happened, but we'll find out when we get down there. Now come on."

They arrived on a floor where everyone seemed crazy, even the officers. Max spoke with Officer Lewis.

She told him what happened and took him into the back. He came out to get Dee. "Look, she's been through something. She still seeing your friend that's dead and she thinks they've taken her away."

"We have to get her outta here." Dee began to cry.

"Look, you have to save the tears, lady. Do you want to see her or not? We can't have you upsetting her, because it will upset the other inmates and it makes it hard for the officers to get them to calm down." Max was irritated.

Officer Lewis chimed in. "Detective, this woman is with child. She can't control her emotions. "Come on, bring that baby over here and get some of these cookies."

Dee was happy to hear cookies, because she did not get to eat the donut Christophe got for her.

Officer Lewis gave her some Kleenex and Max rolled his eyes again. "Can we please get this over with? I need to close this case. I do have other cases I need to work on."

"Hold your pants on. My sweet baby always so serious. Come here and give me a hug. I know you need one. What'd I tell you? Every time I see you I'm going to give you one. You know you need one a day. He hard on the outside, but a puppy on the inside. Don't let his bark scare you. Come on, you get a cookie, too." Officer Lewis handed Max a cookie in a napkin.

Max liked her because she reminded her of his mom. But because he didn't believe in showing emotion, he kept it simple. He smiled and bit the cookie and walked through the heavy sliding door. Dee followed in silence, stuffing cookies in her mouth.

Dee walked up to the room they had Peaches in. She was locked to the wall and she looked beat up. "Oh my God! Why? What happened to her? Get her out of there. Is this how y'all treat people? Like animals? Max, please help her now!" Dee was pissed.

"Yeah, when they act like animals." The cocky man-looking officer who manhandled Peaches walked up to the window.

Dee looked her up and down. "You did this?"

"Yeah, I did." The arrogant officer held her work belt and twisted her mouth like she was welcoming all challengers.

Dee, being a former boxer, eyed her the same way.

"Give me the keys," Max demanded. "She's in a very sensitive state. Why would you do this? And I heard you were asked to stand down and you didn't. And you do her like this?"

The officer handed over the keys with attitude, still staring at Dee.

Max walked in the cell and took the cuffs off Peaches. Dee brushed past the cocky officer and hugged Peaches. She brushed her hair back and kissed her friend's face as tears ran down her own face.

"You need to watch yourself, bitch." The cocky officer threatened.

"No, you need to watch yourself," Max threatened back. "As a matter of fact, you're outta here. Leave or you will be written up and dismissed without pay. I'll make sure of that."

"Dee, where's G-mama? She said the killer is coming for me. She said she wouldn't leave me, Dee, but they won't let me see her." Peaches seemed to be in a daze, laying on Dee's chest.

"Max, please. She's not in her right mind. You know this. Please, can she be placed somewhere better than this? Please." Max knew he probably could, but he thought about the chief and didn't want to make a promise he wasn't absolutely sure he could make good on.

As Dee rocked Peaches and talked to her, Peaches rambled on about memories like she didn't know what world she was in. Dee cried and rocked her friend. She felt immense sadness.

Father of god. I know my faith is not strong, but I call on you in the precious name of your son Jesus Christ. Father, please bring my friend back to her right mind. Please get her out of this horrible place, with these horrible people. Father, I feel like I'm cursed and I have brought this from my childhood over to my friends and surroundings. Please, I will give my life for them. Please God, please. Help them. I promise I will walk away from it all if you please save them. I don't deserve love. I don't deserve them. But they don't deserve this. Please god, please god..."

"Please god, please god." Peaches began to mock Dee.

Max choked up.

Peaches ended, "In Jesus' name."

Officer Lewis walked in and handed Max a card. They walked out and made a phone call. Twenty minutes later they walked back to the room.

"Dee, time to go." Max said quietly.

"No, no, I'm not leaving her with these people. Close the door. Lock us in. I won't leave her to be abused and hurt by these monsters." Dee began to cry again.

"You don't have to. Officer Lewis called in a favor to the judge and they gave permission to have her moved to a state facility where they send officers and government officials. It's a nice place and we feel like we owe her that much," Max expressed sadly.

"I leave when she leaves. They could be lying. No, I won't leave her."

"Baby, I'm going to handle it all myself. I promise you I will get her there safely," Officer Lewis promised. "I have to get her cleaned up, put some fresh clothes on and get her something to eat. I'm off in a few hours, so I will escort her there with the transportation, my love. Once we get there, I'll stay until she gets settled in and I'll call my sweet baby, Detective Max and give him all the details for you."

Dee looked to Max for confirmation. Max nodded his head in agreement.
She kissed a sleeping Peaches on her forehead and laid her down gently. She struggled with her pregnant belly to get up, but finally stood to her feet.

"Come on, my sweet baby." Officer Lewis lent the hand.

Max walked Dee out. When they got to her car, he just stood there until she got in.

"Thank you for everything. I know you think I'm a bad person, but I'm not. I don't know how all these bad things keep happening around me. But you're not what you appear to be either. You're really a nice guy," Dee said as she strapped on her seatbelt.

Max closed her door and stepped back for her to pull off. He walked back in the building to his desk where his little brother stood. They hugged each other with a pat on the back. Without words, he comforted his brother with an unspoken apology.

CHAPTER 15

Biggie woke up with Rob on her mind. She remembered him being there, talking to her one minute and the next minute he was gone.

"Wow, I've been in and out. I wonder if this is normal." She pressed the call button on the remote. "Nurse, nurse, can you come in here, please?"

Missy's nurse came rushing in. "Hi, glad to see you're awake."

"Yes, that's why I called you in here. Is it normal that I keep going in and out like I do? And can you tell me where the gentleman that was here went?"

Missy monitored the doorway, as the nurse spoke with Biggie. "Um, yes, you had a really bad concussion and your body has to adjust to all the medication you were receiving."

Biggie eyes widened in shock. "Oh, really? Well, can you guys stop the meds, because I need to get outta here to help my friends? I have no time to be weak and incoherent."

"I'll talk to the doctor to see what he recommends, and we'll let you know. Other than that, how are you feeling? Do you need anything? Are you hungry? You really need to eat something to feed the baby."

When the nurse walked out of Biggie's room, she shut the door behind her. Missy was right there in her face, so the door didn't catch all the way. The nurse was startled by Missy's abrupt presence.

Missy's eyes were glued dead on the nurse. "What did you tell her?"

"Nothing. She was asking a question and I told her a lie. I really feel bad. I don't think it's healthy for the baby what you're doing. I don't understand. If this is your family why can't she know you're here and why are you drugging her?"

"Bitch, I mean, baby. Look, she's been through a lot and I need to get some information from her and she's not going to give it willingly. You see how strong willed she is. Just a little longer, I promise, then I'm leaving. You trust me, don't you?"

"Um, I don't know. I can get in a lot of trouble if anyone…"

Missy was getting frustrated. "Oh boy, you're not going to get in trouble. Do you trust me or not? Or is it I'm only good for kissing and eating that pussy?"

The nurse's face turned beet red, then blank. The head nurse stepped off the elevator. She looked around for her staff. She was tall white woman with a strong walk, good posture. She looked like she took hardcore aerobics and yoga.

Missy didn't understand the nurse's face change. "What?"

"The head nurse is here. Walk away before she sees you." The nurse adjusted her uniform.

"Excuse me, you two. Come here, please. Who's working this desk and why is everything in a disarray?" The head nurse questioned.

Missy tried to walk away, like she wasn't speaking to her.

"Excuse me, nurse, I'm speaking to you too." The head nurse called out to her.

Missy turned around slowly. "Me? Oh I don't work here. I'm here visiting a family member."

Biggie heard the voice outside her door and felt a familiar connection to the voice.

At the same time, Mo, the dietician walked off the elevator to bring lunch for the patients on the floor.

"Oh, forgive me. You both are wearing the same scrubs. You can see how it was confusing."

Mo went to the front desk to check in on that floor. "I see y'all two working together again today?"

The nurse quickly changed the subject. "Oh, I see you have your dreads pulled back. They look nice like that."

"Oh thanks. Yeah, we have to dealing with food. They are very strict down stairs. So like I was saying, the girl you work with, is she seeing anyone because I was thinking of asking her out?" Mo questioned.

The head nurse was trying to catch up, but she was confused. Missy said she didn't work there, but this worker obviously believed she did. But she didn't say a word. She walked behind the desk, acting as if she was checking on patient files and continued to listen.

"Um, I don't know what you're talking about. I have a lot of work to do. Our other nurse is on lunch and this is no time for conversing. People are hungry, so please stick to your job." The nurse was rude to Mo because she was trying cover her butt and, she was also jealous.

When Mo walked into Biggie's room, she was pissed at how the nurse had spoken to her. She was talking to herself aloud. "Man, some of these people off the hook."

"I'm sorry." Biggie thought she was speaking to her."

"No not you, just thinking out loud. Excuse me." Mo cleared her mind to do her job.

"That girl that was by the door, do you know her? Her voice sounded very familiar."

"Which one? It's three ladies out there." Mo was confused.

"Never mind. I deal with so many nurses I can't keep up." Biggie shook her head.

Mo served her and moved on from room to room. When she hit the last room on the left corridor Missy was in there with a patient that was in a coma.

"Hey, there you are. How are you? I was starting to think you were avoiding me. I saw you when I got off elevator, but you were moving too fast and when I asked your girl at the desk about you, she acted as if she didn't know what I was talking about. So what's up with you?" Mo was being very flirtatious to let Missy know she was feeling her.

Missy was already on it and flirted back. "Oh never avoiding you, baby. And don't pay her no mind. She's just a dingbat, don't know if she's coming or going."

The nurse was doing her rounds and heard what Missy said to Mo about her. It hurt her feelings. She thought Missy really liked her and was confused by her actions. But she also feared her and didn't want to confront her again, so she walked to the next patient, until they came out of her coma patient's room.

"Would you like to get a drink tonight?" Mo did not waste any time.

"Sure, um, but…"

"But what? Oh shit, you're seeing someone else. You got me playing myself." Mo grabbed her heart in play.

"No, that's not it. I'm working on something right now, and I want to finish it up tonight. However, if I get what I want tonight, maybe we can meet for breakfast at Shaw Dairy in the morning." Missy smiled seductively.

"Cool, you got my number. Call me." Mo smiled back and went on with her work.

The nurse saw Mo leave. She walked in the room where Missy was still hiding out.

"You know you can't hide out in here forever. The head nurse is going around to check on all the patients," she said with attitude as she checked her patient's levels and machines.

"Okay so, she doesn't know if this is my people or not. What's wrong with you? What's with all the attitude?"

"Nothing. I've been thinking. No, I don't trust you and I don't want to do this anymore."

"What? Oh you don't trust me? Good, you shouldn't. I knew you would pull this type of shit on me. Let's go out here and tell head nurse what the fuck it really is." Missy grabbed the nurse's arm and pulled her to the door.

"No, no please. I'll get fired and I don't want that on my record. Please don't!" She began to cry.

Missy knew she had to move fast before she got caught up. "Don't cry. Come here. Give me a kiss."

Missy pushed the door all the way closed. She shoved the nurse against the sink and deep tongue kissed her. She rubbed her breasts while she unhooked her bra from the front. The nurse, still crying, didn't stop her. She knew it was dangerous. Missy sucked on her breasts, slurping and slobbering them down as if they were not in front of a patient.

"Please don't. He's right there," the nurse moaned.

"He's in a coma. Shit let him wake up and watch. He might enjoy it," Missy said as she pulled the string on the nurse's pants.

She pulled her pants down, softly kissing the pubic of the nurse. She snatched her pants in aggression. She threw one of her legs and planted her face deep into her pussy.

"Aaaahhhhh oooooohhhh shhiitt." The nurse grabbed her mouth with her free hand.

Missy licked and sucked the nurse's pussy, while slowly fingering her up against the sink. "You really don't trust to me, baby?" Missy got in the nurse's head.

"Yes, yes. Uuumm, yes, I do." The nurse moaned and bit her lip.

"Look at me! Don't lie to me because I eat this pretty pussy good. Tell me the truth. I'll leave you and find someone else to fuck. Is that what you want? Huh? Tell me you want me to stay with you." Missy began fingering her harder and deeper.

"Please don't leave me. Stay with me. I love you. I trust you. Oh shit, please stop. I'm going to scream. Please stop. Don't stop. Oh my gggggggooooooddd! I'm about to cum." The nurse bit her lip until it was red and burning.

Missy pounded her finger in and out of the nurse's pussy like a jack hammer, until she could feel the nurse's pussy tighten. Then she snatched her finger out and sucked her clitoris until the nurse came all on her face, jerking and convulsing as if she was just hit with a taser.

"Shhh, shhh. You're okay. Now be a good girl and don't make me spank that ass. Okay?" Missy warned then kissed and fondled the nurse a little more.

"Okay, I'm sorry. It's just the dike girl asked about you and the pressure of the head nurse being here, it's all getting to me." The nurse apologized.

"Don't let it happen again."

"Okay." the nurse replied passively.

Missy grabbed her face again. "No, I mean it. I would hate to have to kill you. And you say, yes daddy from now on."

The nurse gathered herself and tried to walk away.

Missy grabbed her. "What I say?"

"Yes... yes daddy." The nurse felt degraded. She knew that Missy was dangerous and no good for her, and if she did not get away from her, she was going to end up really hurt.

CHAPTER 16

Through the window, the head nurse watched and saw everything. As they came out the room, she moved backward into another patient's doorway in just the nick of time without them seeing her. Carrie the nurse had left the room with her head down and Missy with a look of anger. Carrie the nurse walked to the front desk and sat down to gather her thoughts. Missy searched around for the head nurse, so she could sneak back into Biggie's room and find out what she knew and where Peaches was. Just as she turned to check the back hallway, the head nurse stepped out the doorway.

"Are you looking for someone in particular, or can I help you with something?"

"Um, no, I was just taking a walk and stretching my legs." Missy cleared her throat nervously.

"Oh really?" The head nurse gave her a skeptical look.

"Yes, sitting in these chairs all day really gets to you." Missy smiled.

"Well, let's see what we can do about that. Follow me." The head nurse turned to walk away with a swing in her hips.

Missy smiled thinking to herself, *This lady is flirting with me.* She followed the head nurse to the big office. When the young nurse looked up to see them walking her way, she jumped up.

"Is something wrong!" Her voice was loud and nervous.

The head nurse smiled. "No, this visitor needs a more comfortable position. Have you finished all your rounds?"

"No, I was waiting on you." The nurse still nervous spoke to the head nurse, while staring at Missy.

"You can finish without me. Nurse Carr should be back soon. I can handle things up here until then," the head nurse ordered.

Just as she spoke, Nurse Carr walked out of the elevator. The young nurse walked away in fear of getting in trouble. Nurse Carr placed her bag under the desk and went to check on her patients.

The head nurse walked into the big office with Missy on her tail. The office was big and had a few roller recliners. "Have a seat. Does any of these work for you?" the head nurse asked.

"Anyone will do." Missy smiled a sexy smile.

"What kind of nurse are you?"

"Oh, um, I'm not a nurse," Missy stammered. "Oh, the scrubs? Yes I used to be a nurse, but I… not… anymore… but they are comfortable to sit around in."

"Um hmm. Why are you here?" The head nurse sat at the end of the desk looking directly into Missy's eyes.

"I told you why." Missy thought to herself. *This bitch knows something. I'm going to have to kill her.*

"Yes you did, but I don't believe you. As matter of fact, I know you're lying. Because the coma patient whose room you were in has no family, and no one has ever signed in to see him," she said, walking toward Missy.

Missy didn't say another word.

"Tell me, how long have you been fucking my nurse?" The head nurse inquired with a side eye.

Missy still didn't say a word.

The nurse took off her lab coat, threw it to the side, and pushed Missy's sexy little body against the door. "My next question is have you ever been with a real woman?"

Missy pushed the head nurse off of her. She pushed her down in one of the recliners. "I knew you wanted me to fuck you. I can always tell. Don't ever put your hands on me."

She walked up to the head nurse and pushed the recliner all the way back. She looked around the room and grabbed a long, round glass candleholder, shaped like a dildo, and put it in her mouth. Missy got down on her knees, pulled the head nurse's skirt up to her waist and her lace panties down to her ankles.

"If these panties hit the floor, I'm going to fuck you in your ass hard as fuck with this, do you understand?" Missy demanded.

"Yes," the head nurse panted.

Missy was impressed by the head nurse's well groomed pussy. She kissed her pussy nice and slow. The head nurse began to cum instantly. "Wow, it's been a long time since you've been pleasured. I know it. What? Are you married to a dead dick motherfucker who don't know you like to have your pussy eaten by women?" Missy smirked.

"Yes."

"Well, I'm going to eat your pussy, suck on your pussy and finger fuck your pussy so good and then you're going to be mine. Do you understand?"

"Yes, yes!"

Missy did just that. She enjoyed it more because the head nurse wasn't such a boss when her legs were up in the air. She moaned and groaned and came three or four times. Missy finger fucked her in her pussy and in her ass. The head nurse rotated her panties hit the floor.

"Didn't I tell you not to let the panties touch the floor?"

"YES!" the head nurse screamed as the glass object surged into her ass.

Missy did not care. She fucked her hard as she could with that candleholder, pushing it deeper and deeper into her until they both came. The head nurse screamed so loud Nurse Carr knocked on the office door.

"I'm fine, just knocked something over."

Missy got up off her knees, sat over in another recliner and took a deep breath. "I'm not leaving this floor and I'm not visiting. I have something I need to find out from one of these patients and then I'll leave. But until then, I'm not going anywhere."

"Okay, look, I don't normally do this at work. I saw you and the nurse and I haven't had it in so long, I couldn't control it."

"I don't give a fuck and don't say okay to me. Say *yes daddy*." Missy was cold.

"Yes daddy." The head nurse liked everything Missy was giving her.

Missy rolled her eyes and got up, pushing the chair into the coma patient's room. As she passed Biggie's room she noticed she had a visitor. It was Dee. She knew she needed to get close enough to hear what they were talking about. She stopped pushing the chair and stood outside the door.

"They had her handcuffed to the wall and she was beat up and bleeding, I didn't know what to do. I wanted to go crazy on somebody." Dee shared her experience visiting Peaches.

"What precinct, first?" Biggie inquired.

"Yes, that's where Max works."

Missy's eyes widened. She smiled deviously and rubbed her hands together. "Found that bitch, yes! I think I have a chick that works down there who owes me a favor."

"Excuse me, nurse," Dee walked to the door and saw Missy.

Missy quickly grabbed the facemask she wore around her neck and grabbed for the recliner again.

"I'm sorry, I'm busy. Push the nurse call button for the nurse at the front desk." She then whispered, "I don't fuck with you hoes."

"Excuse me. What did you say?" Dee questioned, not sure if she heard what she thought she heard."

Missy moved on down the hallway as if she didn't hear her.

Dee walked out the room to the front desk, asking for ice and ginger ale. But no one was at the desk, so she went into the mini kitchen area and looked for herself. Missy watched her walk into the kitchen. When she no longer could see Dee, she got her needle out and prepared another treat for Biggie. This time, it was more than the normal dose.

"Goodnight, whore. You and your bastard baby going to take a long nap." Missy smiled to herself.

She slid into Biggie's room and acted as if she was checking her machines. "Okay, time to clean your lines," Missy whispered.

Biggie got an attitude. "No thanks, I think y'all keep telling me y'all cleaning my lines, but you are really giving me medicine. And like I told the other nurse, I'm trying to go home. I don't want any more meds."

"Look, I'm only doing my job, and you don't get a say. The doctor makes that decision." Missy tried to keep her cool.

"Fuck you and that fucking doctor. I'm not taking any more meds and that's that!" Biggie got as loud as she could.

Missy snapped. "You stupid little bitch, you deserve to die!"

Biggie reached up and grabbed for the needle that was coming at her, but she accidentally grabbed the facemask instead. Her reflexes were off from being doped up so much. Missy tried to stab Biggie again with the needle.

"Oh my God, it's you! You crazy bitch, I knew it. HELP!" Biggie screamed.

"Shut the fuck up. You gon' die, bitch, just like G-mama did."

"Dee! Help get this crazy bitch off of me." Biggie tried to keep Missy from stabbing her.

Dee heard the noise, but wasn't sure what it was. She walked out of the mini kitchen and heard screaming. She thought she heard her name, but it was faint.

"Biggie?" Dee called out.

When Missy heard Dee coming, she dropped the needle, ran out of Biggie's room, bumping into Dee so hard it knocked her down. Biggie pushed the nurse's button and the 911 button at the same time on the remote, which sounded a loud alarm. All the nurses began to run toward Biggie's room.

"What's going on?" the head nurse ran to help Dee off the floor.

All the nurses and hospital security were now in Biggie's room, asking her questions.

"Dee, it was her! She told me she killed G-mama and she was trying to kill me too, with that needle." Biggie pointed to the floor.

The security picked it up. Biggie explained all that happened.

The head nurse and the young nurse didn't say a word.

When Missy hit the bottom stair, she opened the side door, which led to an exit, but she had to go through the diner and cooks station to reach it. When she hit the last door, she rammed into it with all her might. The light from the alley hit her with a puff of smoke.

"Hey you, where you going in such a hurry?" Mo, the dietician, was leaning against the wall having a sneak smoke break.

Missy's heart was racing and Mo's voice out of nowhere scared her. "Um... um, look, I need your help. I have an ex after me and I saw her upstairs. I think she saw me. She's trying to kill me. I need to get outta here. Can you help me? I'm so scared of her." Missy was looking around because she knew it was only a matter of time.

"Yeah, I got you, baby. Let me clock out. I'm almost off the clock anyway." Mo stepped in the doorway, swiped her card, and they walked down the alley to her car.

CHAPTER 17

Jeremiah finally got his phone call. He called a lawyer friend of his that worked with him at the firm.

"Willard, we were wondering where you were. It wasn't until this morning I saw your name come up on file. What happened, man?"

"Wait, you saw my name come up this morning and I had to call you? You should have been down here to get me out," Jeremiah said angrily.

"Hold on, damn it! I'm not your errand boy. The boss is on everyone's ass today because you've been MIA. Also I've been in court handling some of your cases and mine."

"Look, muthafucka, let's not forget you owe me. You wouldn't be able to do our cases if I hadn't taken the bar for you. Yes, remember that? And it's not about you being my errand boy. You're supposed to be my friend. Have my back. You haven't heard from me in a week. It never occurred to you to check on me? No, I guess not. With me out the way, you're first in line to be top dog, right? Well guess what, muthafucka, you could never be me."

The lawyer whispered into the phone. "Damn, man, you really going to bring that up? You're the top dog in the firm, and yes, you did me a favor, but I don't owe you shit."

"Jeremiah's voice heightened like a gangster. "Fool, how you figure that? I took your test for you, I covered cases for you, and don't think I don't know about you packing cases to win them."

"Uh, what?"

"Yeah, uh duh. What is right. Now get down here and get me out this hell hole!" Jeremiah demanded.

"I'm on my way," his friend replied sadly.

~~~~~~~~~~~~~~~~~

Once he reached the jail, he paid Jeremiah's bond and waited from him to come out. Jeremiah retrieved his belongings and asked for his paperwork. He wanted to get all the information he could on Max, so that he could make sure he'd never work again.

Jeremiah was throwing his weight around as a law officer and being aggressive as he was being released. The officer that was handling him listened to every word he said without saying a word.

Once Jeremiah was out the door, the officer called up to Max's desk to let him know Jeremiah bailed out and that he was talking about how he was going to handle Max and Christophe.

"Max, he's lawyer. He works for a big firm. You better watch out and be careful, I don't know what this dude has done to you, but don't be the normal hot head. I been down with you too long and I know when you do things like this, it's never a good thing," the officer pleaded with Max.

Max chuckled. "It'll be all right. Thanks for looking out. I'll be in touch."

Jeremiah went through his belongings in the car. He made sure everything was there. "Look, I need your help. I need you to find out everything you can about this detective for me."

"Why? Who is he and why do you need me to do it?" His co-worker David questioned.

Jeremiah got on the phone and called his assistant, as if David wasn't speaking to him.

The assistant answered. "Jeremiah Willard's office. How may I help you."

"Denise, what the fuck? How is it you went a week without seeing your boss and you don't do a search for him?" Jeremiah laid into her.

"Sir, I've been calling your phone for days and I've been to your house. I've been trying to cover for you. I thought you took a time out to be with your fiancé. I've been with you since day one. With all due respect, I've been with you from day one and I've seen you do some peculiar things, and I've always backed you. But please don't expect me to know what's going on in your life every minute every day. I have my own family that I have been missing out on, here covering for you. You have a million messages. All the partners are in an uproar, and your clients are burning a hole in the phone lines. Now, are you on your way in from lala land?" Denise fired right back to him.

Jeremiah rolled his eyes and looked over to see Dee's shop was jumping. "What the fuck? Stop, stop!"

"Sir, I've asked you..." Denise began.

"Shut up, Denise. Not you. I'll call you back."

"But sir, the partn...."

Jeremiah hung up on her as she was speaking. She heard the dial tone before she could finish her sentence.

David was tired of Jeremiah ordering him around. "What is it now, Willard? Why are we stopping?"

Jeremiah jumped out the car. "This bitch going on with her business while I'm locked up because of her fuckery?"

David pulled up and parked the car with no idea that what was going on.
Jeremiah walked in the shop, busting the door open so hard it broke the glass in the frame.

Chrissy spun around in fear but with attitude. "What the hell's your problem?

"Where the fuck is Dee and who the fuck are you?"

Chrissy put her hands on her small country frame. "Who the hell are you and what do you want with Dee?"

One of Dee's up in age clients was sitting in Chrissy's chair. "Oh shit, no, no, no. It's him. He's the one that came up in her before, putting his hands on these girls. Not today motherfucka!" She pulled her gun out her old lady bag.

Jeremiah put his hands up. "I'm just looking for my fiancé."

David ran to the door in disbelief at what he had just saw his co-worker do.

Chrissy chirped her fireman husband. And all the clients stood up and gave them that you-don't-want-what's-coming-to-you look.

The client with the gun said, "Now you got that shit off before you liver lip motherfucker, but I came prepared this time and you ain't gonna get Dee. And you ain't gon' hurt this pretty little white lady right here."

She grabbed her cane and began to walk closer. "Now, I suggest you bid us a goodnight and you and your partner move on 'bout ya business."

The receptionist looked at Chrissy and mouthed good night. Chrissy shrugged her shoulders and watched Jeremiah and David back their way out the door.

When they were walking to the car, Jeremiah noticed Dee's truck coming down the street. He took the keys from his co-worker. "Get in. I'm driving."

"Dude, I don't know what's going on with you, but I want no parts. Willard what is wrong with you? Are you trying to lose everything you worked for?" He got in the passenger seat of his own car, talking to Jeremiah but Jeremiah wasn't listening.

Jeremiah pulled the car out and to the side of the plaza. He watched Dee come down the street, park her truck, and walk up to her shop.

When she walked up, she could hear reggae music coming through the door. Shoot Out by Mykal Rose. Once she got closer, she saw all the glass broken from the door.

"What happened?" she asked. She was already drained from what happened at the hospital. Everyone in the shop began to speak at once.

"Your baby daddy came up in here trippin'" someone said from the back.

"He broke the door and cursed out your workers," someone else chimed in.

"Yes and Mrs. Harlem Nights here saved us when she pulled her gun out on him." Chrissy joked to lighten the mood.

"What? He was here? Did anyone get hurt? She pulled a gun? Oh my goodness." Dee could hear everyone's voices and replied to all of them at one time like she had super powers.

Dee looked toward the door to see if she could play out the event in her mind. She wondered if he was still out there and was waiting for her to get here so that he could come back in to try to hurt her again. Chrissy's husband and a few of his friends walked in the door in a hurry and frightened her out of her thoughts. She thought Christophe was with them, but was disappointed when she saw that he wasn't.

Jeremiah refrained from coming in. He was just released from jail and needed to get himself cleaned up and back to work, so he could see what his next move should be.

"She want that pretty boy fireman? She could have him, but I'll make sure she'll never be happy again. And she's not going to have my baby around some lame punk. It's me and our family or misery forever, bitch!" Jeremiah spoke out loud from a dark place within him.

CHAPTER 18

Big Rob had been visiting Peaches in the institution for the last few weeks. She did not seem to be getting any better and she spoke of G-mama all the time, which pissed him off. The kids were back at home and really needed their mom so he continued to try to deal with it, although he thought of Biggie daily. He wondered about her, about their baby and why he hadn't been to see her in weeks like he knew he should.

Peaches and her nurse walked in the room and distracted his thought.

Nurse Jasmine said, "Hello, Welcome back. She's not talking too much today. She's been real quiet, but when I told her you were here, she asked about her children. Maybe you can talk about that. I mean, I know this is still a correctional center, but maybe it'll be good for her to see the children to help snap her back. I like to see all the inmates get better and hope they'll go home to their families."

Rob faked a smile. "I'll think about it."

She removed the cuffs from Peaches' hands and walked back into the hallway. Peaches sat at the table and stared out in the open space. She was not the same woman Rob had married. Although he was still pissed with her, it hurt him to see her like this. Rob reached over to grab her hand, but Peaches jumped in fear.

Rob knew why. "Peaches, the kids ask about you all the time. They really want to see you. I told them you were away at college to get some extra education. They colored some pictures and told me to bring them to your school."

Peaches did not respond.

Rob pulled out the coloring and pushed the pages across the table.

Peaches looked down at them and began to cry. She missed her babies, but she could not really remember their faces. She picked up the papers and began to cry deeper.

"Why? Why can't I remember them? Why can't I remember you? G-mama said I'll be all right, but she won't come back. Why did she leave me? No, please don't bring my children here to see me like this. I'm crazy and fucked up. The lady I share a room with screams out all night that she's being raped by her father. It's torturing. The man down the hall is looking for his dog. He's been looking for his dog for 10 years, he says. He's only been in here for six months. My hands won't stop shaking, even if I hold them between my thighs. Please don't bring my children here to see me." Peaches cried into her hands.

Big Rob began to cry from seeing Peaches' tears. He could not believe this was his wife. He felt sorry for her and did not know what to do. For the next hour, they sat there in silence until the visit was over. Once the nurse came back in to get her, Peaches jumped up and walked away without even a goodbye. Rob wiped his face and walked out into the hallway.

He waited to be released from the building and decided he needed to check on Biggie. He called the hospital and they told him she had been released. He didn't just want to stop by her home due to the fact he didn't know who would be there, so he called her cell.

"Hey you." Biggie answered.

"Hey you. Wow, it feels so good to hear your voice. Why didn't you tell me you were released?" Rob asked.

"Why didn't you try to find out? I hadn't heard from you in a while and due to your situation after finding out about Peaches, I figured you needed to take care of that first. Plus, I really didn't know how to talk to you about this. But I think of you all the time." Biggie smiled.

Rob bowed his head with a smile. "Can I come see…"

"Yes! "Biggie answered before he could finish his question.

Rob chuckled. "I'm on my way."

~~~~~~~~~~~~~~~~~~~

Dee had not heard from Christophe in weeks. She wished she hadn't told him to go away, but she knew it was the right thing to do because of her situation. With the love she held for him in her soul and his in return, she wouldn't be able to concentrate and turn whatever bad spirit that laid upon her around. Plus, she couldn't go on if another love of her life was hurt because of the curse she believed was around her. The more she thought of him she began to feel him close to her. Her thoughts became deeper, so deep she almost fell asleep. She could smell his cologne and feel his hands touching her body. She turned around and the vision of him in her doorway seemed so real.

"Dee, I love you." His words whispered to her.

As he walked up, he wrapped his long, strong arms around her pregnant waist. She gasped for air. Looking up into his beautiful brown eyes, Dee did not say a word. She allowed his thick luscious lips to kiss her softly, then deeply, until she almost lost her breath.

The passion between them was strong and powerful she did not want it to end. He slowly moved down to her neck, kissing her and nibbling on her slowly. Meanwhile, he slowly removed her clothing. His mouth opened wide for her full, supple breasts. Dee rubbed her hands slowly over her breasts, down her stomach and to the top of her pussy. She could hear Christophe speak. "Can I taste you?" his imaginary words made he shake. She shook her head and came back to reality. She couldn't under why she was having these day dreams about a man she barely knows, but she has to stay focus.

She had been visiting Peaches regularly and there was no real change with her situation, which made Dee very sad, but she seemed comfortable where she was and Dee was happy about that. Although Biggie was home, she still did not know how to deal with her because they still had not spoken about what she was going to do about Big Rob and the baby.

Dee felt like things were too quiet. She was not leaving anything to chance. She spoke with Det. Max daily, never asking about Christophe, but figuring if Max didn't bring him up, he must be doing well. She was determined to find the bitch that killed G-mama and get Jeremiah out of her life for good. She hadn't heard from him or seen him, but she knew he was around. She needed to get back to the shop. With all that was going on she felt as she was not giving her shop the attention she should, she decided to make a stop up there.

On her way to the shop, she called Chrissy to as if they needed anything.

"Heavenly Hands Beauty Salon," Chrissy answered in a country professional tone.

"Hello, beautiful. Hey, why are you answering the phone? Where's your receptionist?" Dee questioned.

"Dee! Hello, my dear. Oh she's in the back loading the towels in the dryer. What can I do you for?" Chrissy smiled in her voice.

"Well, I'm on my way in and I wanted to know if you ladies needed anything?"

"Why yes, sweetie. I missed breakfast this morning. Hey y'all, this is Ms. Dee. She wants to know if y'all need anything.?" Chrissy yelled with the phone still to her mouth.

Dee took the phone from her ear before Chrissy blew out her eardrum.

"Food," one of the girls yelled out.

"Yes, food. I don't care what as long as it's good," the receptionist yelled from the back.

"Everyone wants food. "Chrissy gave Dee the message as if she couldn't hear everyone yelling in the phone.

"Okay, is there anything specific?" Dee smiled

"Oh, yes. Real food. No Mickey D's for me. You know that little restaurant that cooks hearty food down on Shaw? My hubby goes there often, even though it's out our way. He loves their loaded grits. What's the name of it? Dairy Place? Dairy something?" Chrissy tried to guess.

"Shaw Dairy." Dee chuckled

"Yes, he loves that place, down in the hood as he calls it. And Janelle's. He says they have the best service and the best BLT he's ever tried." Chrissy said, thinking about her husband.

"All right, I got you. Everyone else said whatever. Is that whatever I order for you too or do you want loaded grits and bacon." Dee smiled

"That's exactly what I want. Thanks, sweetie pie. See you when you get here."

~~~~~~~~~~~~

As Dee walked into the diner, she saw someone jump up really fast and move. She was looking into her phone, checking her social media, so the sudden movement kind of startled her with all that has happened. But she dismissed it. As she was placing her order she felt a weird feeling like someone was staring at her. She turned to her left and a young dyke girl with dreads was giving her the onceover. Dee thought to herself, "*Sorry, honey, strictly dickly.*"

She rolled her eyes and looked back at her phone.

The girl cleared her throat. "Excuse me, don't I know you?"

Dee tilted her head with attitude. "No, honey, I don't think so."

"Yes, you used to come visit your people in the hospital. I'm the dietician that brings her food most times.

My name is Mo. I'm actually with one of the nurses she had. I think she went to the restroom. She jumped up so fast I didn't really get where she was going," Mo went on.

"Oh, yes, okay. Please excuse me. My mind is all over the place. Had a bad experience in that hospital. I can't think clearly on people I meet right now," Dee apologized.

"Yeah, I understand. As a matter a fact, Missy had a bad experience too. She quit that same day," Mo continued.

The waitress called to Dee. "Sweetie, your order's up."

As Dee grabbed for her bags she played back what Mo just said to her. She let her mind stand still for a moment. She recalled the person she saw out the corner of her eye jumping up and running to the back. She let her mind go in slow motion for a minute. "It's her! What did you say her name was? Where she go?" Dee began to dial Det. Max's number.

Mo and the other customers were confused. Dee tried to run in the back, but one of the waitresses stopped her. "Ma'am, you can't go back there. Employees only."

"But a woman ran back there. She's a murderer. I have to catch her." Dee was out of breath.

"Murder!" Mo yelled out.

"Miss Shirley, did a girl run back there?" the waitress yelled in the back.

"You know what? I do believe somebody did. I was bent over in the oven. I felt something blow past me, but I brushed it off as the heat from the oven. I didn't pay it no mind, child." Miss Shirley said, creeping out the back, wiping her hands on her apron.

Dee fell down in the seat at Mo's table. She could hear Max on her phone in the distance of her thoughts.

"Dee, Dee? Can you hear me? Where are you?" Max yelled once more.

She put the phone up to her ear. "Shaw Dairy," she managed to whisper.

Mo got up to walk out. "Can I have the bill please?"

"Where do you think you're going? You have to stay here until the detective gets here. He's going to want to talk to you."

"Yo, I know my rights and I ain't did shit wrong. Hey, he can talk to my lawyer." Mo threw money on top of her bill and chucked up the deuces.

"Wait, please. I need your help. Look, this girl is dangerous. I need to know how you met. Have you been to her place? Do you have a phone number? Please stay. She might have murdered my friend, my family and I could be next, or maybe you. If you haven't done anything you have no need for a lawyer." Dee held Mo's arm.

Mo thought about it for a minute. She really didn't know this girl and the last thing she wanted was the cops walking in on her at her work, asking her questions about a murderer. "Yeah, all right, but I don't know what good it's gon' do. I really don't know much about her. Damn it, I need caffeine. Yo, excuse me." Mo sat down and signaled for the waitress to fill her coffee cup up.

Det. Max walked in with two Cleveland Police officers. "Dee, you good? What happened?"

Dee was eating. "Yes, she was here. She saw me come in and jumped up and ran out the back."

"Does anyone know which way she went?" He looked around the diner.

"No, but she was here on a date with this girl. She works as a dietician at the hospital Biggie was in. I asked her to stay here to speak with you."

Dee's phone rang. "Hello? Chrissy, I'm sorry. Something happened. I'll explain when I get there."

"Are you all right? He didn't try to get you, did he? Honey, you need to call Christophe. He's really worried about you and he'll protect you." Chrissy had sympathy in her voice.

Dee was happy to know Christophe was thinking of her as much as she was thinking of him, but she knew it was the right thing to leave him alone right now. She also knew Max would not approve and she really needed his help.

She smiled. "Chrissy, we'll talk when I get there."

Max took Mo off to the side with one of the beat cops and began to take her statement. Mo swallowed hard. "First, let me start off by saying I haven't done anything wrong. I was going to send y'all to my lawyer, but I'm cooperating."

Max did not say a word.

The beat officer said, "And we thank you. Let's hope your information can help us out."

"Well, I met home girl at the hospital a few weeks ago. I had never seen her before and I thought she was hella fly, so I offered to take her out. I gave her my number and flirted with her a few times. After that I think she was kicking it with this other lil honey on the floor, a nurse, because every time she'd see me she'd give me the mug face." Mo chuckled.

The officer said, "Um, the mug face?"

Max explained. "She balled her face up."

The officer shook his head. "Oh yeah, yeah right. I gotcha. Go on."

Mo continued. "Yeah, so I didn't pay too much attention. Anyway, so one day I'm down off the back entrance from the kitchen sneaking to smoke a spliff. Wait, this not gon' get back to my job, is it?"

The officer shook his head no.

"Cool. So the door busts open hard as fuck. Man, I thought it was my boss and I was busted. I see it's shorty, Missy. She looks like someone's chasing her. I asked her if she was okay. She said some chick she used to fuck with was after her and she needed my help. My shift was almost over, so I told her to go sit in my car over in the outside lot and I'd be there in a few. I asked my boss if I could clock out early and go to my car. When I get to my car shorty's laying down on the back seat. She looked crazy scared, yo. She said she couldn't go home and she was scared of being alone, so I took her back to my place. That's where she been ever since. I go to work and leave her in my place. She never talks about anything, where she lives or nothing. I call my house phone when I want to talk to her and she said she likes her privacy so I give it to her. And she mad sexed up."

The beat officer asked, "Mad sexed up?"

Max answered. "She's a freak."

The beat officer replied, "Oh yeah, yeah. I gotcha."

"So, yo, shorty a murderer? For real, yo?" Mo shook her head back and forth.

"She's a suspect and you're the only witness we have right now to know her last whereabouts, so you are too." Max gave her the cop eye.

Mo jumped up. "Wait, what? Nah, nah. I gave y'all the information I know and y'all can go to my house. I don't fuck around like that. I'm out. Y'all want to talk to me again? Call my lawyer."

Max said, "We'll do that. You make sure you call him first."

He let Mo leave. He believed she was telling the truth. He just wanted to scare her a little bit in case Missy did show her face around, Mo would be willing to turn Missy in.

After he got all the information he could, Max told Dee to be on her way. There was nothing else for her there and if he found anything he would let her know.

Dee grabbed her cold food she picked up for the shop and walked out to her truck. She decided to call Biggie to fill her in on what happened.

A man answered the phone.

CHAPTER 19

All of the other partners gather themselves in Jeremiah's office waiting for him to come in. When he walked by his assistant's desk she tried to warn him.

"Sir, before you go in there…" She handed him a folder and his coffee.

Jeremiah brushed her off with attitude. "Not now. I don't want to hear it."

He walked into his office to the ambush and became outraged before anyone spoke a word.

"What the hell is this?" He walked over to his desk, placed down the coffee and the file.

"Willard." The voice of the head partner was stern.

"We've been informed of your arrest. And we're here to get to the bottom of all the mess that's been going on in your life for the last few months. You are a mess, young buck, and this is something we do not need or want in this firm. Baby mama drama or whatnot." He pointed his finger at Jeremiah. "You're a partner, Willard. You should conduct yourself as such. We all peek under the rock sometimes. Most of us have wives. However, we like to pick at the weeds every once and a while. But you know as well as anyone else does: you go down in the gutter and play with trash, it'll get in your eyes."

Jeremiah sat in his high back soft leather chair, crossed his legs and folded his hands in his lap. He stared at his co-worker who had obviously ratted him out.

The head partner continued, "Now, it's seems like you have a lot to clean up. We have that big merger this afternoon. We're meeting our clients a Marciano's and we need you to close it out. However, after it is closed, we suggest that you take a leave of absence until you get all your personal business taken care of and can handle the business. David will handle all of your cases until you return.

Jeremiah stood up and walked to the front of his desk. He sat down on the edge and folded his arms. "Frank, don't ever call my fiancé` trash. She's pregnant with my child. I've done damn good work for this firm, made y'all a lot of money and gotten a lot of great cases. I am a partner. You can't ask me to take a leave of absence. I won't. My personal life doesn't have anything to do with what goes on at this firm."

"That's where you're wrong. Everything you do in your life has everything to do with your position here. You look bad, we look bad. If your clients cannot get in touch with you, and we can't get in touch with you when your anger has driven you to react in such a way it affects the firm. You are and you will take a leave of absence or suffer the consequences. You're a damn good lawyer. Young, hard working and smart. Don't make a mistake you will regret later." The head partner walked up to Jeremiah and grabbed both of his shoulders.

All the partners walked out. David stayed behind to defend himself. Jeremiah stared at David all while the partners excused themselves.

When they were all out, he clapped his hands very slowing three times.

"So, you sold me out, huh? It's understandable. When you can't be as good as me, you get me out the way to come up. I didn't know you were that smart, David.

You surprised me." Jeremiah stood up and grabbed the letter opener off his desk.

David didn't notice it as he defended. "Look, I didn't sell you out. You sold yourself out. You have it all, man ,but you gon' let your anger allow you to lose it. The partners knew about your arrest before I told them anything."

Jeremiah grabbed David by his tie and pushed him against the bookshelf in the corner of his office. He put the point of the letter opener to his throat.

"You think I'm going to let you get away with this shit? I can ruin you and you know it. If you touch any of my cases, I will make sure you will never try another case again."

David could not breathe or speak with Jeremiah holding his tie so tight and poking him in his throat. Jeremiah released him and pushed him toward the door. "Get the fuck out my office."

"Willard, you better take you own advice as warning." David choked out while rubbing his throat and adjusting his tie.

~~~~~~~~~~~~~~~~

Max took the time he had free to stop by the fire station to visit his little brother. He knew Christophe wasn't taking the rejection from Dee well and, of course, he was happy about it. Still, he did not want his little brother to hurt. He thought about the thing Christophe said about their parents as he drove. He thought to himself, *"Love gets you nothing but heartache."*

He shook it off. He didn't want his mind to wander off to a love he lost. When he pulled up to the fire station, he parked in the fenced parking lot. He saw a few of the other firemen out washing the fire trucks.

"Yo, Max in the building!" William Powers yelled out, running up for a hand shake.

"Sup? I see y'all working hard. Where's your cut off shorts and heels?" Max gave all the guys a slap five and half hug hand shake.

Everyone laughed hard and said, "We saved that part for you. The grimy work is for the cops."

"Yo, where is he?" Max walked and talked.

"He's been in the gym all morning. For the last couple weeks, he's been all work and work out. See if you can bring him out his funk. It's hard to play a joke on my homey when he stops laughing," William contested.

Max went through the side door and up the stairs through the mess hall across a long bridge walkway until he reached the gym room. He could hear the weight from the universal weights clinking to his brother's workout.

"Don't tell me they got y'all being soft up in here using these Curve weights," Max teased Christophe as he hit the corner of the gym room door.

Christophe stopped his motion when he heard his brother's voice. "What do you want?" He began his reps again.

"Wow, is that the welcome the fire department gives when a man comes to check on his lil bro? Who pissed in your Cheerios?" Max poked his brother in the ear, making him drop the cord for the pull weight.

"Yo, stop playing." Christophe hated when his brother did that.

Max chuckled. "C'mon bruh, what's up? I know you're better than this. Look, she made her decision and it was the best decision for you. I mean, her. Look, she has too much shit going on with her."

Christophe shook his head. "I know she didn't want to do it. I feel the love she has for me. She's missing me right now and she won't answer my calls or nothing."

"Well, look at it this way. She loves you too much to let you get hurt, and when she has cleared up all the drama around her, I'm sure she's going to give you a call."

Christophe looked at his brother with eyes of optimism. He couldn't believe of all people, he would hear those words come from Max's mouth, and because it was him to say it, he believed it.

"Thanks, bruh. I really needed to hear that." Christophe smiled and hugged his brother.

Max grabbed the back of his brother's head. "Now can you please take off the panties and let's go downstairs and beat the heels off these fools in some b-ball."

"I don't know. I don't think you can hang, big brother," Christophe teased.

Max took a folded towel off the counter and threw it at his brother. "Let's find out."

"Wait, what happened with the girl from the restaurant? Did y'all catch her?" Christophe was worried about Dee.

Max shook his head. "No, not yet, but you know I always get my man, well woman in this case. Shit, it's not even my case, but I told ya girl I would do everything I can to help her and I plan to stand by my word."

They headed downstairs and the guys were ready for them. Max took off his leather jacket, threw it to the side, and took point guard position. The testosterone filled the room these guys were playing like they were in the NBA. Running up and down the court, playing mad defense and sweating up the floor. Each team making point one after the other. They were playing hard.

So hard the ball got trapped on top of the ladder truck and William climbed on top to get it. All of the guys were sweating and panting, waiting for the ball.

One of the guys said with a deep scratchy voice, "Hey you guys up for some drinks later? We're going down the street to this bar where all the nurses hang out. I plan on playing doctor tonight."

Christophe looked at his brother for confirmation.

Max thought for a second. He really never took time to hang out, and right now his little brother needed him. He could take an hour or so for a drink a two. "Yeah, I'm in. Show y'all fools how to mack."

William laughed. "Mack? That's 1996. Bruh, no one says mack anymore."

Max smirked. "Well, I do. This is why I get the ladies and you young heads strike out."

Christophe and William bucked their eyes. They laughed, but they knew Max was dead serious. Some of the older firemen agreed with Max, but most of them were married, so it didn't mean too much to them to join in the debate.

~~~~~~~~~~~~~~

Once the guys showered and headed to the bar, the nurses were already turned up, happy to be off work and ready to drink away the hours of the hospital. A few of the firemen knew some of the nurses, so when they walked in the ladies screamed, "Fire!"

Those guys ran to the dance floor and Christophe, Max, and Williams headed to the bar. The barmaid walked over to them and said, "Two firemen and a cop walk into a bar…"

They guys looked at one another. Christophe and William wore their firemen T-shirts so, of course, they knew why she fingered them. But they wondered how she knew Max was a cop.

The barmaid continued. "Sounds like the opening line to a filthy bar joke, right?" She laughed a sexy, angelic laugh.

Max straddled the stool in front of her and said, "I'm not a cop, but just how does that joke end?"

She smirked. "Yes, I know you're a dick, I mean, detective. Now you're wondering how I know."

Max was intrigued.

She leaned over the bar and whispered, "Because it's my duty to know, officer. Oh and the joke would end with you getting laid. So, whatcha boys having?"

William laughed. "Yo, Max, looks like you just got macked. Let me get a Heineken, please."

"Ooh, a gentleman with manners, and you two?" She never took her eyes off Max.

Christophe ordered the same.

Max finally responded. "You seem to know so much, surprise me."

The guys were having a good time. After a few drinks they all started to get turned, except for Max. He noticed a young nurse in the corner. She didn't look like she was there to have a good time. She seemed to be hiding away in the corner as if she was looking for someone or watching someone. She had the same drink she ordered hours ago and she was almost invisible.

The barmaid walked up behind him. "Checking out baby in the corner?"

Max turned to her without saying a word.

"She's been coming here for a while, but these last few weeks she's been different. She sits in that corner, orders her drink and watches the door for hours, like she's waiting for someone. After awhile she finally drinks the drink and leaves.

Max smirked and turned back to the little nurse. "So, who do you think she's looking for?"

"A lover." The barmaid smiles, tops off Max's drink and walks away.

Max shook his head and looked at the guys on the dance floor having a great time. He was happy to see his little brother enjoying himself. He hoped that this would take his mind off love for a while. Just then, he saw Miss Invisible buck up. He followed her eyes to the door and there was a young, sexy girl standing there. His eyes went back to Miss Invisible. She straightened her hair and sat up straight, trying to be noticed by this weaved down, sunglasses in a dark club, sexy little thing. But she never looked her way.

She walked over to the bar, sat on the stool next to Max, glaring around as if she was looking for someone.

The invisible nurse strolled down to the bar and walked up to the sexy diva. "I knew you would come. I knew you would be looking for me. I went to your apartment. I've been calling you, but I knew you would be looking for me sooner or later. I miss you so much…"

"Sorry, do I know you?" The sexy diva dismissed the nurse like they had never met.

The nurse couldn't believe it. She had a pale dead look on her face. She wanted to cry, but did not want to appear weak. She said, "I gave you my body. You said you love me and you can sit here like you never met me and ignore me? How could you?"

The sexy diva turned her stool toward the barmaid. "Sex in the driveway, please?"

Max and the barmaid gave each other the eye. The nurse didn't know what else to do, so she ran out the door with tears running down her face.

Max turned his stool toward her, not recognizing her at all. "Wow, that was harsh. So I see you're the love 'em and leave 'em type, huh?

She turned her stool toward him and gave a flirtatious smirk. Then she saw the badge on his waist. She turned back to face the bar. "Maybe!"

"Wow, am I that ugly, you had to look away that fast?" Max teased. He actually liked her attitude. It kinda turned him on.

The barmaid walked up and told them she was buying shots. She laid out eight shots glasses, poured 151 in them, and set them on fire. "What's your name, sexy lady? You up for the challenge?"

"Missy! Yes always." Missy smirked and grabbed a shot glass one by one and took them to the head.

When she reached the sixth one, she looked at Max who watched her with impressed eyes. "What about you, handsome? Are you going to let a lady drink alone?

Max smirked at her challenge and drank the last two.

All the firemen were on the dance floor having fun. Christophe and William were dancing with twins. The barmaid lined up eight more shot glasses. She poured the liquor, set them on fire and turned to put the bottle away.

Missy stood up on the stool and grabbed her arm. "Leave the bottle."

Her and Max took turns taking each shot to the head. Missy held on to the bottle and went for another round.

The DJ slowed the music down. He played "Earned it" by The Weeknd and Missy got up from the stool and began to rotate her hips and whine dance. She slowly raised her arms in the air and seductively brought her hands down over her face, down her neck, and to her breasts.

Max was truly turned on by the way her body moved.

Christophe watched his brother from across the room and smiled. He hadn't seen his brother enjoy the presence of a woman in a while. He tapped William on the waist and nodded over to the direction of Max.

The way that Missy was dancing made many eyes turn in her direction. It was sensual and very enticing. Max couldn't resist her. However, he had a gut feeling that told him something was wrong. Missy walked over to him very seductively and began to dance for him. The DJ changed the song to a reggae song, "Wine Slow" by Gyptian. She looked him in his eyes and rubbed her hands slowly down his chest as she rocked her hips in between his legs. She turned around and bent over and slowly rolled her ass as she sat down on his lap. She leaned back into his chest and whispered in his ear. "Do you like that, baby?"

Max licked his lips and positioned his cop exterior to hold her up without saying a word. Missy turned toward Max, pressing her hips into his crotch, grinding and throwing her hair back and forth softly and sensually.

The smell of her perfume and the sexiness of her exotic moves aroused him in a way he couldn't control. She climbed onto his stool, straddled the stool, and grinded her pussy into his waist. "Is that a gun in your pocket or are you just happy to see me?"

Max wrapped his hands around her waist, jumped up and held her up. Missy wrapped her legs around his waist and kissed him deeply.

The barmaid watched them in lust, wishing it was her. She grabbed the almost empty bottle and went to put it back on the counter. She saw something floating in the bottom of the bottle. She put the bottle up to the light over the showcase and she recognized the floater was a "sunshine pill" (X). She turned toward them and Missy was kissing Max and looking the barmaid in her face.

The barmaid leaned over the bar and tapped Max on the shoulder. Missy slid down his body ready for the drama. Max turned to see what the barmaid wanted.

She asked, "Can I play?"

Missy smiled and said, "Yes, can she?"

Christophe didn't know what was going on, but he was surprised to see his brother showing public affection to a girl in a club. His brother didn't seem off, so he didn't think too much of it. It was just nice to see Max having a good time for a change. He sat at the table next to the dance floor and went to his Facebook page and posted a love poem.

Max gave a dazed look. "Yes!"

The barmaid looked at her co-worker on the other end of the bar. "Yo, I'm out. See ya tomorrow."

The co-worker frowned and threw his hand up in the air.

The threesome left the bar without a goodbye.

Missy didn't know what she was doing with this cop, but she knew she needed something under her sleeve. Since she couldn't find Mo and the nurse was too in love, she had to move fast. However, she was not moving smart. She took Max and the barmaid back to her apartment. What she didn't know was that the nurse followed them there. She was in love with Missy and when she saw that she was having a threesome, she became overly jealous.

Max was so drunk and high, he was all the way off his mark. His penis was thinking for him. And since it had been a while for him, the only thing he could think about was sex.

The barmaid drove max car, since she was the only sober part of the group. When they reached Missy's apartment, Max kept looking over his shoulder and so was

Missy. She knew why she was, but she wondered why he was doing it.

"What's up, sexy? You're having second thoughts or something?" Missy picked his brain.

Max staggered a little bit. "No, not at all. I just had a strange feeling we were being followed."

"Don't worry, that's just the X…" the barmaid almost gave it up when Missy gave her a sharp eye.

"I mean, the ecstasy and excitement building up in you." The barmaid cleaned it up.

Missy grabbed Max's face and deep tongue kissed him. They fell against the door of the downstairs entrance. Max grabbed her ass and pulled her in closer, lifting her up in the air. The barmaid grabbed Missy's keys and opened the door. They made their way into the apartment still kissing, groping and grinding on each other.

The barmaid put her purse and the keys down on the table. She looked around Missy's apartment. It looked like it hadn't been lived in for a while, but she looked past it. She walked over to the two of them, removed Max's jacket from behind. As he and Missy devoured each other she stood on the couch and began to nibble on his ears. Max reached his left hand around and rubbed her ass and the back of her thigh. She pulled his head back away from Missy and began to kiss him. Still standing behind him on the couch, she kissed down his neck. He was still facing Missy. Missy opened up his button down shirt and began kissing his chest and moving down to unbuckle his belt. Max took his hand and gently started rubbing the barmaid's pussy through her pants.

"Ummmm," the barmaid moaned.

When Missy unbuttoned Max's jeans he stopped, looked down at her with his sexy brown eyes, licked his lips and grabbed her face.

Missy pulled his thick, long dick out of his boxer briefs. She looked at it. The room was silent. They could only hear the rhythm of their breaths and heartbeats fill the room. Missy couldn't believe how big his dick was.

The barmaid stepped down from the couch, gave Max the up-down and smiled at Missy. She got down on her knees next to Missy and kissed her in the mouth. Missy moved back from her and looked deeply into her eyes. The movements were slow like a daydream, but the passion filled the room. The barmaid licked her lips then deep throated Max's dick into her mouth. Max grabbed her hair with pleasure.

Missy pulled her mouth away and kissed her. Then she deep throated Max's dick. They both put their hands on his dick and began sucking and kissing on it. Max couldn't take it. He fell back on the couch, but this did not stop them. These ladies sucked and licked his dick, his balls and swallowed his nut as he came repeatedly.

Missy let the barmaid have the dick after while because she wanted to taste her more than suck dick.

So as the barmaid gave Max service, she opened the barmaid's legs, moved her thong to the side and began to kiss on her pussy. The barmaid moaned deep on Max's dick as Missy ate her pussy. This made Max moan, feeling the vibration from her throat. He looked up and watched Missy finger fuck and eat the barmaid out.

He loved it. Missy looked up at him as she devoured the barmaid. He was so turned on by it, he got down on the floor and began removing both of their clothes. By now, the barmaid and Missy were going at each other's body like animals. They were in a sixty-nine position and Max was watching them while rubbing his dick up and down, wondering who he was going to have first.

Missy, who was on top of the barmaid, made the decision for him. She sat back on the barmaid's face, opened the barmaid's legs and rubbed her clit. "She's ready for you, officer. Put that big dick wherever you want to." The barmaid was still licking Missy's pussy from the bottom.

Max did not say a word. He climbed between her legs, dick hard as a rock, and put the head of his dick into the barmaid's tight, throbbing pussy. He could feel her cumming on the head of his dick.

As she moaned, Missy sat her pussy harder on her face and grinded her hips hard almost suffocating her. "Push that big dick in that pussy and fuck the shit out of her. Please, daddy, please."

Max pushed his big, long dick deep into the barmaid and deep kissed Missy and began to fuck the shit out of her. The barmaid couldn't breathe or move. She tried to push Missy off, but she was not in a position to move. Max had her legs and Missy was straddled over her arms and face. Her pussy was soaked with her wetness and her face was soaked with Missy's juices.

Missy finally got up, turned to her and kissed her. "Do you like that? Say yes!"

The barmaid did not know what to say. She was a little scared, but she wanted this so she went along.

Missy walked away and came back with a strap-on. Max was still fucking the barmaid. "Save some for me, officer," Missy said as she rubbed lubricant on her dildo.

Max was confused, but he went along.

She grabbed the barmaid by her hair and rolled her over. Max laid down on the bed and the barmaid was on top of him. Missy was controlling this union like only she could and she enjoyed every minute of it.

"Ride that dick!" she ordered the barmaid who was weak from Max fucking the shit out of her.

Max, still under the influence, didn't really realize what was going on.

As the barmaid worked her pussy on him, he threw his head back and let her have full control. Missy came up behind her and slowly slid her middle finger into her ass. The barmaid tightened up on Max's dick. He liked the feeling.

Missy worked her finger in and out of the barmaid's ass feeling her wetness and tightness. "Relax and let us have you. This is what you wanted, right?" Missy whispered in her ear.

"Yes, yes, yes." the barmaid moaned.

Missy grabbed the back of the barmaid's hair and removed her finger then pushed her dildo slowing into the barmaid's ass. It was short and thick so Missy moved very gently.

The barmaid tried to relax, but with the thickness of Max in her pussy and Missy in her ass, she couldn't help feeling like she was being conquered.

Missy reached around the barmaid's neck and lightly choked her from behind and worked her dildo into her ass. Max fucked her from the bottom while Missy worked her from the top.

"Please, please I can't take it!" the barmaid screamed and moaned, but she grinded her hips to the both of them.

Max grabbed her face and deeply kissed her in the mouth. He whispered in her ear. "Ride this dick."
She was sweating and panting. Her pussy juices flowed down on him and out her ass like never before. She begged for them to stop, but her body was responding and asking for more.

Max flipped them over and pulled Missy's dildo off. He laid them on top of each other and slid his dick into Missy's tight pussy. She was much tighter than the barmaid. As soon as he entered her, he began to cum. He pushed his dick deep inside of her and bit down on the barmaid's breast.

Missy yelled out in pleasure. She loved the feeling of him deep inside of her as the barmaid laid on top of her. But he wasn't finished. He fucked from her to the barmaid, taking his dick in and out of both of them. The barmaid rolled over and let him at Missy and it was like she was watching a porno. Missy and Max flipped, scratched, pulled, fucked, kissed, fucked, bit, and rode one another like they were long lost lovers.

The barmaid walked to the kitchen to get something to drink when she saw a shadow move in the corner of the hallway. "Hello, is someone there?" She got a scary feeling in her spirit. She moved back in forth in the light coming from the window. "Maybe it was my own shadow," she chuckled. "Damn, they wore me out."

She headed to find the kitchen.

Missy couldn't believe she was enjoying sex with this man, but he was fucking the shit out of her and she loved every minute of it. She even let him kiss her in the mouth. She sucked his dick. Something wasn't right about this, but she didn't want it to end. She rolled over on top of him and pinned his hands down over his head. She looked him in his eyes then she caught a glimpse of her peeping in the door. Missy smiled.

"So you can't stay away, huh? You know I'm dangerous, right?" she said as she looked Max in his eyes.

"Yeah, well, I'm a big detective. I think I can handle it." Max smiled, thinking she was talking to him.

But the nurse was in the apartment watching them from the doorway. She knew Missy was talking to her. She was so in love with Missy she hated to see her with them. She backed up in the corner of the dark doorway. She didn't know what to do.

The barmaid was heading back to the room with a glass of ice water. The nurse couldn't go back the way she came and she was too scared to make a move toward the room. She panicked.

"Stop!" she yelled. "You shouldn't be fucking her. She's dangerous and she'll hurt you!" The nurse jumped out the corner into full view in the doorway of the room.

It scared the shit out of the barmaid. She dropped the glass of ice water and it broke at her feet as she screamed.

Max jumped up. "What the fuck? Who the fuck are you?"

Missy reached over, grabbed a tall copper candleholder on her nightstand and bashed Max over the head, knocking him out cold.

The barmaid stood naked, in shock, with ice and glass around her feet.

Missy jumped up and grabbed the nurse around the neck. "Bitch, didn't I tell you it was over? You trying to get me fucked up?"

"What the fuck is going on?" the barmaid stared at Max's limp body laid across the bed.

"Wait a minute, wait a minute. Yo, you have to help me tie him up and …"

"And what? This is a detective and I don't even know you. I was just looking to have a good time, but you have killed a cop. I'm outta here. Oh no no no. This is bad. This is really, really bad." The barmaid cried out as she grabbed all her clothes, trying to make a run for it.

But Missy wasn't having that. She hopped over the bed and walked up on the barmaid with the candleholder in her hand. She grabbed the barmaid. "Look, bitch, you wanted in, so you're in. If it wasn't for this stupid turned-out bitch, we wouldn't have to do this shit. But I need to get him tied up so I can think and you're going to help me or be lying beside him. You choose."

Max's phone began to ring. All of the ladies paused, looking around at one another. Then all eyes were on Missy.

CHAPTER 20

Big Rob was telling Biggie about his visits with Peaches. Biggie could see the sadness in his eyes. She held his hand as he vented. "You know what? I'm sure you'd rather be talking about something else. You looking much better. Can I get you anything?" Rob smiled at Biggie.

"Actually, I would like to get out this house. I was wondering if you could take me to the shop. I would love to see someone familiar and I would love to see Dee." Biggie smiled.

Rob knew it was not a good idea for him and Biggie to be showing up together at the shop, but he couldn't tell her no after everything that has happened. He helped her gather her things and held her hand as they walked out to his truck. Minutes later, they were headed to Heavenly Hands. He figured he'd drop her off and then go to visit Peaches again. This way, Biggie would have time to talk to her girl.

~~~~~~~~~~~~~~~~~~

Once they reached the shop, Dee ran out to meet them and help Biggie out of the truck. Because she was still sore from her bruises and weak from some of the medications. She looked at Big Rob and didn't say a word. He gave her a look as if he didn't care. He walked around to Biggie. "I'm going to see Peaches and then I'll be back for you in an hour. Are you cool with that?"

Biggie bowed her head in embarrassment. She gave Dee a side eye and put her arms around Big Rob to assure him it was okay.

Dee and Biggie slowly walked into the shop so that she could meet all the new ladies and see how the shop had been remodeled.

"Chrissy, this is Biggie." Dee introduced Biggie walking her into the shop holding her hand like she didn't want her to ever let go.

"Oooohhh, come on in here. I've heard so much about you. Aren't you sweet? How are you feeling, baby girl? I feel like I know you already." Chrissy made Biggie room to get comfortable.

Biggie looked around and looked up at where her station used to be. She felt a little jealous that these women were in their space. She then looks over at Dee and could tell she was hiding something.

"What?" Biggie asked.

"What, what?" Dee rubbed her belly, continuing with the silence.

"Something is on your mind. I know you. Is it because Big Rob dropped me off?"

Chrissy jumped in with her country accent. "No, not at all, sweetie. Look, just because you got pregnant by your girlfriend's husband, doesn't mean she feels some way about you. She's been through a lot with her crazy fiancé` and falling in love with Christophe. Then there's the crazy lil girl that tried to kill y'all and Peaches being locked up in the looney bin…"

Another girl added her two cents. "Speaking of lover man, he's parking his truck. I think he's here to see you, Dee."

Dee's eye widened. She was overwhelmed with thoughts. She really wanted to see Christophe, but she knew she needed to keep him at distance. She tried to think fast, but she had no clear thoughts that could give her a way out.

Biggie looked back and forth from girl to girl and back to Dee. "Dee, what the fuck is going on?"

Christophe sat in his truck and dialed his brother's number again. He didn't know what happened to him after the bar. Max left without saying goodbye. He still got no answer and the call went to voicemail. He decided to call his desk. He happened to look up and saw Dee standing in the door of the shop. He put the phone down

"Detective Maxwell's desk. Hello, hello? Is anyone there? Hello."

Christophe thought to himself. *Damn she's beautiful. How could any man ever want to hurt her, or walk away from her? I have to tell her I love her; I have to tell her I'm never leaving her side. I want to be with her and will help her through all of this.*

He never hung up his phone. He opened his truck door and could feel Dee's eyes on him. She could feel and a see his eyes on her. Both their minds traveled away as they watched one another through the glass door.

~~~~~~~~~~~~~~~~

Meanwhile, when Big Rob walked into the clinic to see Peaches, the nurses and orderlies were having a party for the patients, but Peaches was still in her room in bed.

"We tried to wake her, but she's been very quiet and in her feelings this week, so we try to leave her to herself," a nurse confessed.

They headed to her room. Once there, the nurse opened the door to a sleeping, limp Peaches. Big Rob shook his head and stood there as the nurse went in to check on Peaches.

Peaches' eyes popped open. "What? What you say, G? Oh no. Help Biggie. Help Biggie!"

"What? What the fuck you saying? What happened to Biggie? What the fuck are you saying?" Big Rob shook Peaches so hard her head flipped back and forth like a rag doll.

Peaches head dropped to the side. "Don't let her die, G. We have to all be together. Don't let her die, please."

Rob jumped up, ran out the room and pulled his phone out his pocket to call Biggie.

Biggie stood up gingerly and walked her sore body to the door to see who her friend was head over heels for. "Damn, he is beautiful. Dee, what is the problem?"

The rest of the ladies high fived. "Yes, that's what we keep telling her. I would jump his bones two times."

"Me too." The other stylist said

Chrissy stood on the other side of Dee. "What'cha gon' do, girl?"

Dee reached for the doorknob.

Christophe started around the street.

The ladies smiled and squeezed each other's hands in excited, hopeless romantic thrill. Dee walked out the door like a teenage cheerleader waiting for her high school crush when she saw a car coming toward Christophe full speed. Her eyes darted at the car and then at Christophe.

She moved as fast as she could, waving her hands back and forth. "Stop, watch out!"

Christophe heard her, but it was all happening so fast he only could hear the tires screeching.

Biggie saw the car and saw Dee heading to warn Christophe. She hobbled out the door to get Dee out the way.

The car was inches away from Christophe.

Dee leaped out to push Christophe out the way.

"Dee, nooooooo!" Biggie grabbed Dee from behind and plunged her to the ground from the back of her dress, which was too much for Biggie in her current state. She fell back and hit her head on the concrete. The car slammed hard and the horn sent out a lingering roar.

Then everything went quiet.

All you could hear is heartbeats.

Smoke from the car filled the air.

The ladies ran from the shop, seemingly in slow motion.

Blood was everywhere.

Chrissy quickly called the fire station. "Babe, come quick…"

Christophe's phone was lying in the middle of the street. The detective who answered Max's desk phone heard everything.

"Please don't die. Please, please I need you in my life. I love you. I can't live without you. I can't take it. I can't…"

CHAPTER 21

Missy and the barmaid tied Max up. The nurse had already called the cops. The nurse thought to herself. *"If I can't have you, no one will. You'll be in jail and need me to take care of you."*

Missy grabbed the nurse and threw her against the wall. "What is your fucking problem? Didn't I tell you to beat it? I got too much shit on me to be dealing with your thirsty ass. Don't you get it? I used you, bitch!"

The nurse cried. "You're a, you're a bad person. You hurt those people. You really did it. You killed that girl, didn't you?"

Max began to wake up. He tried to reach his hand up, but realized he was restrained.

Missy put her hand around the nurse's neck. Rhinestones on her gel-covered nails twinkled in the light. "Yeah, I did it. That bitch was supposed to love me. She fucked me and loved another bitch, and when I get rid of all of you, I'm going to kill that bitch Peaches too!"

The barmaid backed into the corner as tears ran down her face.

Max's eyes widened in disbelief. His phone began to ring again. He noticed that the GPS tracker light was on. It showed cops that if they're in harm's way, the station is trying to locate them. He didn't say a word; he just listened.

Missy raised the copper candleholder up in the air ready to smash the nurse over the head.

BOOM! BOOM! BOOM! BOOM! Loud knocks sounded on the door.

Missy jerked her head toward the bedroom door. "What the fuck?"

The barmaid jumped out her skin and slid down to the floor.

Max looked up at her and mouthed, "It's going to be okay."

For some reason she instantly became calm.

"You bitch! You set me up!" Missy choked the nurse harder.

The nurse's eyes began to water. "Plea…"

"Missy Cassandra Brian, we know you're in there. We know you have one of our men. Open the door or we will be forced to break it down," the lead officer threatened.

Missy dragged the nurse to the living room of the apartment. She whispered to her, "Tell them if they come in here, everyone will die."

The nurse cried.

"Tell them! Tell them now!" Missy demanded.

"She… she said if you come in here, we'll all die," the nurse cried through the door.

"Are you okay? Is anyone hurt? Where is the detective?" the officer replied.

Silence.

Missy panicked. "Fuck you! I won't give up. You'll have to take me dead. I won't come. I want…"

"He's alive. He's hurt, but…" the nurse tried to warn them.

Wham! Missy hit nurse Carrie over the head with the candleholder.

The barmaid and Max were still in the bedroom.

"Untie me," Max whispered.

"No, she'll kill me. I don't want to die, not like this. I just thought you were beautiful and wanted to have a good time. I can't..." The barmaid cried.

"I won't let that happen, I promise. I will protect you. Look, this chick obviously needs some serious help. If you don't, she's going to come in here and kill us. I know she's killed before. She's part of a case I'm working on. Fuck!" Max suddenly made a realization. He started to put it all together.

The barmaid cried into her knees.

"Look at me. Untie me. I promise I will get us outta here." Max looked at her with sincere eyes.

She began to untie him. It was hard because they used duct tape and it was wrapped super tight. When she was almost done, Missy came in the room dragging the nurse and saw what the barmaid was doing. She dropped the nurse and ran toward the barmaid.

"You bitch. No!"

Max jumped up and kicked her in the face. The barmaid curled up in the corner.

Missy hit the floor head first, knocking her dizzy.

Max grabbed his pants, put them on, and yelled out, "Come in. Come in now!"

The team used the boot and busted opened the door. Officers filled the apartment.

Missy scrambled to get to her feet and grabbed the knife she dropped, but Max was on her ass before she could give a clear threat. He punched her in the face, slammed her down on the ground and dragged her to him by her left arm.

"It's over. You're going away for a long time."

The lead officer stood over her with his gun to her face. "Missy Cassandra Brian, you're under arrest for kidnapping, resisting arrest."

Max added, "And murder!"

They cuffed her and walked her out to the patrol car.

Max walked up to the barmaid and reached out his hand. She was still curled up, shaking in fear. "Do you want my hand to fall out?"

The barmaid looked up. Officers and EMS personnel were everywhere. She reached up and grabbed Max's hand. He pulled her up to him face to face and he became very dizzy.

"Help me down to EMS truck, please."
She smiled and assisted him.

The nurse was on her way to emergency. As Max got patched up, the detective that answered his phone walked up to him. "You're always somewhere with all the ladies." He teased.

Max shook his hand and laughed.

"When we found out you were here and the call came in, I wanted to come and warn you about your brother."

Max jumped up from the EMS who was treating him. "My brother? What about him."

"I don't know exactly, but this is the address we traced." The detective handed Max a piece of paper.

Max snatched the paper, read it, and rolled his eyes. "That damn shop. I should've known."

Max ran to his car, he was so glad the barmaid drove it. He jumped in and took off. "I warned him to stay away from her. I'm going to put an end to this right now."

CHAPTER 22

When Big Rob pulled up, it was worse than he imagined it. Blood was everywhere. Police cars, EMS, and fire trucks were blocking the streets.

Christophe had Dee cradled in his arms. Her head hung back and blood was streaming from her head and through her pants. "Please, baby, don't die. I love you. My parents told me when you feel the zing that is your forever love. I know you are it. This isn't the end. Please don't leave me."

Biggie sat off to the side of him, rocking back and forth.

Big Rob ran over to her. "Baby, what happened? Yo, you a'ight?"

The ladies in the shop all were standing around crying.

The other fire fighters were trying to get Christophe to let them check Dee out. "Bruh, please let us help her. We need to see if she's still here for you and we have to check the baby and get her to the emergency," William pleaded.

Christophe got up and carried her to the EMS. A trail of blood followed them. They told him to walk away, but he wasn't having it.

Her body started to react. She began to go into cardiac arrest.

Biggie screamed and ran toward the truck. The ladies and Big Rob grabbed her.

Christophe jumped on the truck and onto Dee and began pumping her chest. "Pull off. Pull off now! We need to get her to the ER. Come on, Dee baby, stay with me. Please stay with me."

The other EMS guy pulled on Christophe's shirt. "Please let me help her."

Christophe fell back and cried like a baby.

~~~~~~~~~~~~~~

Back at the scene, the car was empty.

"We need to find out who this car belongs to. I want it swept for evidence and brought back to me ASAP," the chief bitched.

Max pulled up and jumped out his car. "Where is he? Where is my brother? Is he okay? What happened? What happened to my fucking brother? I told him to stay away from this bitch. If she got my brother hurt, I swear..."

William stepped up. "Bruh..."

Biggie screamed out. "If that bitch? Who you calling a bitch? She's never a bitch. He loves her and now she might be dead and you're screaming if she hurt your brother? Fuck you and your brother!"

"No, fuck you. Where is he?" Max walked up on her aggressively.

"Max! Get your ass over here now!" the chief demanded.

As Max walked over to her, the car in question sparked fire. All the cops and detectives grabbed whatever they could and ran away before the flame blew into a roaring fire throughout the car.

"Fuck! My evidence!" the chief screamed out.

She walked up to Max. His face was in shock. "I don't give a fuck what you have to do. Check street cameras, theses assholes' phones, but find out who was driving this fucking car and find out what your brother's girlfriend has to do with it. You understand?" She hit Max in his chest.

Max stared at the fire in deep thought.

"Hey, snap out of it. Your brother's fine, but I'm sure he needs you right now. The girl might not make it. He was really torn about it. Go to him. Then come back and be the detective I know you are. Go, go now."

Max was shock at the chief, she's usually such a hard ass, but he appreciated the consideration. He walked to the shop, apologized to Biggie and all the ladies in the shop. He got in his car and pulled off down the road. He turned around in the alley where a beat up homeless man was. Max turned his car around and took off for the hospital.

The homeless man looked up. It was Jeremiah!

One year later…

Max went into the bar. He walked up to where the barmaid was counting her tips with her back turned. He said, "I was wondering, are you still looking to have a good time?"

She turned around and said, "For the guy who saved my life? Sure."

Max smiled. "Do you think you can have a good time at a BBQ today?"

"Maybe. I get off in an hour. Why don't you sit down and have drink until then?" she said with a love spell smile.

They both laughed and talked for the next hour.

~~~~~~~~~~~~~~~~~~~

You could hear the baby crying from the driveway. Once in the house, it was in surround sound.

"What are you in there doing to my niece? Don't worry auntie's coming. C'mon lil Dee, auntie got you. Your mommy being mean to you? Biggie, don't be making auntie's niecey poo cry and mess up her pretty face." Dee went on as she walked in the room.

Biggie looked tired, like she hadn't slept for days. "Girl, your niece has been changed, fed, rocked, kissed, loved on and all that mess and she still won't stop crying. I don't know what to do. You're so lucky you don't have child…"

Dee's eyes averted to the floor.

"Dee, I'm sorry. Oh no, I'm so sorry. I'm on no sleep. I don't know what I'm saying. Please forgive me."

Biggie spoke before thinking, forgetting Dee lost her baby the day she pulled Christophe out the way of that car.

The kids were running through the hall. "Mama, mama he's trying to hit me."

"Little Rob, stop chasing and trying to hit your sister." Biggie yelled out the nursery.

Dee smiled. "Wow, they call you mama? I must say, you are doing really well to be raising Peaches' kids after her suicide. I still can't believe it. With everything that happened, how has this affected the kids?"

Biggie stared off into space. "They're up and down. I pray about it each and every day. I didn't like a lot of what Peaches did, but I loved her. Now I'm married to her husband and raising her children, with a child of my own by him. I keep waiting for God to strike me down. It's a challenge each day."

"So, they say the suicide letter said she found out about you guys and that's why she hung herself?" Dee questioned.

Biggie was in tears. "Girl yes, it said she wanted to go be with the only true person that loved her, G-mama! What we still want to know is how she found out." Biggie sniffed. "The day we went there to tell her is the same day we found her hanging there. Crazy thing is, they said she had a visitor, but no name was on the list. And they still haven't released the videotapes."

"Dee? Dee, baby, y'all coming down or are we going to have a bar-b-que up in the nursery?" Christophe teased.

Dee wiped her tears and smiled. "They must need our help downstairs. That's the only reason they would be calling us down."

Biggie laughed and wiped her tears as well. "Rob always wants me to get the kids, do something in the kitchen or bring him something."

As the ladies came down the stairs, Max and his date were pulling into the driveway.

The ladies peeked out the window, then at one another.

"Don't even think about it." Christophe warned.

"Think about what!" both ladies said in unison.

Rob looked at Christophe and they both walked away.

Max walked in through the house with a large envelop in his hand. Dee, still holding Davida or "lil Dee" as everybody called her, walked through the kitchen and to the patio. Everyone followed.

Max waved the envelope and grabbed the barmaid's hand. "All right, before I introduce my date, I have some very important information. We finally received."

Biggie waved her hand back and forth. "Hell no, I don't think so."

The barmaid laughed. "Right, I'm Ebony."

"Okay, now that that's done, you can grill her later, Biggie," Max continued.

Biggie rolled her eyes and looked to Dee to confirm she'd have her back in that grilling session.

Max and the guys shook their heads.

"We finally received the information we were waiting for, footage from the video cameras at the institution, and they were right. She did have a visitor."

Max handed the file to Christophe. He looked up at Dee and then at Biggie.

"Who? Who was it, baby?" Dee held the baby tight.

Christophe turned the file to them and said, "Jeremiah!"

1. Who is your favorite character and why?
2. Do you have "uglies" or crazy drama at the beauty salon you go to? Or have you heard about any shop drama?
3. Do you think it'll be a part 3 to this series?
4. Do you have "uglies" or crazy drama at the beauty salon you go to? Or have you heard about any shop drama?
5. How did this book effect your outlook on life and in your relationship?
6. Would you read more of Ms.BBC upcoming work?

Please leave reviews on www.amazon.com, or www.facebook/Ms.BBC presents Uglies Of The Beauty Salon

Ms.BBC a native of Cleveland, Ohio founder of BBC PROMOTIONS LLC. She became a writer at a very young age. She always had the desire to touch people with her words. And have high hopes to continue to do so for years to come.

Phenomenal Woman
By Maya Angelou
Pretty women wonder where my secret lies.
I'm not cute or built to suit a fashion model's size
But when I start to tell them,
They think I'm telling lies.
I say,
It's in the reach of my arms,
The span of my hips,
The stride of my step,
The curl of my lips.
I'm a woman
Phenomenally. Phenomenal woman, That's me.

I walk into a room
Just as cool as you please,
And to a man,
The fellows stand or
Fall down on their knees.
Then they swarm around me,
A hive of honey bees.
I say,
It's the fire in my eyes,
And the flash of my teeth,
The swing in my waist,
And the joy in my feet.
I'm a woman
Phenomenally. Phenomenal woman, That's me.

Men themselves have wondered
What they see in me.
They try so much
But they can't touch
My inner mystery.
When I try to show them,
They say they still can't see.
I say,
It's in the arch of my back,
The sun of my smile,
The ride of my breasts,
The grace of my style.
I'm a woman
Phenomenally. Phenomenal woman, That's me.

Now you understand
Just why my head's not bowed.
I don't shout or jump about
Or have to talk real loud.
When you see me passing,
It ought to make you proud.
I say,
It's in the click of my heels,
The bend of my hair,
the palm of my hand,
The need for my care.
'Cause I'm a woman Phenomenally. Phenomenal woman, That's me.

www.ingramcontent.com/pod-product-compliance
Lightning Source LLC
Chambersburg PA
CBHW031332170626
46807CB00002B/658